THE STONE FLOOD

Franz Hohler

THE STONE FLOOD

Translated from the German by
John Brownjohn

THE HARVILL PRESS
LONDON

First published with the title *Die Steinflut* by
Luchterhand Literaturverlag GmbH, 1998

First published in Great Britain in 2001 by
The Harvill Press
2 Aztec Row
Berners Road
London N1 0PW

www.harvill.com

1 3 5 7 9 8 6 4 2

© Luchterhand Literaturverlag, 1998
English translation © John Brownjohn, 2001

Franz Hohler asserts the moral right
to be identified as the author of this work

A CIP catalogue record for this book
is available from the British Library

Published with the assistance of the
Swiss Council for the Arts, PRO HELVETIA

ISBN 1 86046 712 1

Designed and typeset in Scala
at Libanus Press, Marlborough, Wiltshire

Printed and bound in Great Britain by Clays Ltd, St Ives plc

The Random House Group Limited supports The Forest Stewardship
Council® (FSC®), the leading international forest-certification organisation.
Our books carrying the FSC label are printed on FSC®-certified paper.
FSC is the only forest-certification scheme supported by the leading
environmental organisations, including Greenpeace. Our
paper procurement policy can be found at
www.randomhouse.co.uk/environment

MIX
Paper | Supporting
responsible forestry
FSC® C018179

THE STONE FLOOD

I

WHEN SEVEN-YEAR-OLD KATHARINA DISCH, ACCOMPANIED by her four-year-old brother Kaspar, arrived at her grandmother's house on Friday, 9 September 1881, she never dreamed that she would remain there until she married.

The children's father had banished them from the inn for a day or two because their mother was about to have another baby. Katharina raised no objection. Her eldest sister, Anna, had packed nightshirts and some underwear in a bundle. Katharina put her wooden doll, Lisi, into one of the folds, making sure that her head was poking out. Satisfied, she took Kaspar by the hand and set off, glad not to have to stay at home.

Her mother had looked very different when they left. She was lying in bed upstairs with her hair spread out across the pillow and trailing over the edge. From time to time she pressed her lips together, shut her eyes tight, and with both hands clutched the bedclothes that covered her swollen belly. She was pale and damp with sweat. Katharina had only wanted to say a quick goodbye from the doorway, but her mother beckoned her over, stroked her head with a clammy hand, and told her softly to give her love to Granny. Someone would bring word as soon as the new brother or sister arrived. Then, drawing a deep breath, she turned over and took a handful of dried plums from the bedside table. "For you and Kaspar – for the walk," she said, attempting a smile. Katharina put the plums in the pocket of her pinafore and stood there in silence, trying to recognise the mother she knew in the woman lying there. "You mustn't be afraid," the woman whispered from the bed, before turning on her back again and closing her eyes.

Katharina stole silently to the door, then raced down the stairs to the taproom. Kaspar, already in his waterproof cape, was squealing excitedly while his elder brother Jakob chased him round the deserted tables and Anna washed up plates and glasses at the sink. Just as Katharina was putting on her own cape, which was draped over a chair, the cat rubbed against her legs and looked up at her, purring loudly. She picked it up, cradled it in her arms, and asked if it wanted to come too. Then, letting it drop, she took her little brother firmly by the hand and said goodbye to Jakob and Anna. "Give Granny my love!" Anna called after her as the children went out into the cloudy afternoon from the door of the Meur, their parents' inn. The cat followed them uncertainly for a few steps, then came to a halt, mewing, with its tail in the air. Looking around for her father, Katharina caught sight of him a little further up the slope, standing beside the haystack on the edge of their meadow. He was holding a scythe with the handle resting on the ground. He waved to them, and Katharina remembered that he'd gone to sharpen the blade.

She looked up across the valley towards the Bleiggen, the fields where her grandmother's farmstead lay, though she

4

knew they were out of sight from here. The track up the mountainside disappeared into the clouds as if it led straight to heaven. Katharina and her family lived on the eastern outskirts of Elm, at the head of the Sernf Valley in the Glarner Alps. This part of Elm was known as Untertal, and lay on the other side of the river from the main part of the village. Whenever Katharina went to school or to church she had to cross the iron bridge that linked them. And anyone from Untertal who wanted to reach one of the mountain passes on the main side of the village had to cross the iron bridge first. It was from this western side, too, that the track to the Bleiggen led uphill.

The two children had only just left home when a crash rent the air. Kaspar, who was frightened of thunderstorms, stopped dead and stared at his sister in alarm.

"Want to go home," he said.

"That wasn't thunder," she told him reassuringly, "it was just a big lump of rock falling."

Katharina couldn't wait to get away from the Plattenberg, the slate mountain that loomed over the Meur, because slabs of rock had lately been breaking off and tumbling down the mountainside. The customers in her parents' inn talked of little else. There was a slate quarry at the foot of the Plattenberg, and the men who worked there often stopped off at the Meur. Katharina liked to sit beside the big stove in the corner of the taproom, scratching words and sums on her slate and listening to what was said. Anna, who had already turned sixteen, waited table while their father or mother stood behind the bar – more often their mother, since the family also had a farm to run. Now that another child was on the way, thirteen-year-old Jakob or their sister Regula, who was twelve, would probably have to help out; but the men preferred a girl to bring them their drinks. Perhaps Regula would serve them and Anna go behind the counter, Katharina thought. Papa would certainly have little time to spare, and he'd already said that the baby was coming at the worst possible moment. Like most of the local farmers he'd been unable to cut a second crop of hay because it had been raining for so long. They were all waiting for better weather.

Katharina couldn't understand why the baby should be coming now, of all times – but then she had no idea how women came to have babies. A man had something to do with it, that much she did know. It was the same with animals. She remembered how vociferous Rhyner's bull had been when he hurled himself at Papa's cow in the meadow this summer. But Papa couldn't possibly have subjected Mama to an assault like that. Katharina slept in the room beside theirs with Kaspar, Regula and Jakob, so she couldn't have failed to hear Papa bellowing. Suddenly aware of this regrettable gap in her knowledge of life, she decided to question Anna on her return. Anna was already a woman – she was bound to know about men because there was one who patronised the Meur for her sake alone: a slate quarryman who also lived on the Bleiggen, in the farmhouse beyond her grandmother's. His name was Hans-Kaspar, and not long ago, when Katharina had been sent to fetch some eggs from old Elsbeth at nightfall, she'd seen the pair of them kissing behind the inn. What if such a kiss could result in a baby? If so, Anna might also give birth to one, but that was impossible because she was still single, and you had to be married to have a child. She must definitely ask her about it, Katharina told herself. Or should she ask her grandmother? No, better not. Granny was kind to her, and sometimes gave her lumps of sugar, but when asked why Grandfather had died, she'd said: "Of a goitre." Her answer to Katharina's next question, "How do you die of a goitre?", had been that she was still too young for such matters. Katharina had no wish to hear that again.

"Kathrinli! Kaspar!" They had now reached the iron bridge, and their sister Regula was coming across it towards them.

"Verena will be over to attend to Mama later on," Regula announced. She had been sent to fetch the midwife, who lived in the row of houses at the other end of the village. Now that old Maria from Steinibach was dead, people sent for Verena Elmer instead, even though she was quite young and had a son too little to go to school. Katharina knew her husband, who often patronised the Meur. He was a mountain guide, and in the autumn he always talked about hunting chamois, but she found most of his stories exaggerated and secretly wondered if even half of them were true. Verena she knew less well because women seldom entered the inn, but she knew that Verena always bound up her plait with a red ribbon. Katharina, who thought this looked nice, wondered why women didn't frequent the taproom more often. Midwives' anecdotes would have interested her far more than chamois-hunters' tall stories.

"There's to be a christening on Sunday," said Regula. "I saw the baby."

"Where?" asked Katharina.

"At Kleophea's."

"What does it look like?"

Regula laughed. "Tiny," she said. "Ever so small, almost like a doll."

"Is it a boy or a girl?"

"Boy."

"This small?" asked Kaspar, pulling Katharina's Lisi out of the bundle.

Regula laughed even more. "No, stupid!" she said. "*This* small!" And she spread her hands to indicate the baby's size.

Kaspar was disappointed. First she'd said it was like a doll, and now it wasn't like one at all.

Katharina took the doll away from him and stuffed it back into the bundle. "Is Verena a good midwife?" she asked her sister.

"She certainly is. Verena's strong – she can even haul a baby out of its mother's tummy by the feet."

"Well, we're going now," said Katharina. She grasped her little brother's hand.

"Bye-bye," said Regula.

In the middle of the bridge Katharina paused and looked down through the railings at the Sernf rushing past beneath them. Swollen by weeks of rain into big brown waves, it was very nearly overflowing. She could hear stones rumbling along the river bed. Or was the sound coming from the

Plattenberg? It wasn't just a rumble; there was a trickling sound as well.

"Want to go," said Kaspar, tugging at her hand.

"No, wait," she said. "Can you hear the stones bumping along the bottom?"

"Come on," he insisted, tugging harder.

"There's no need to be afraid," she told him. "The bridge will hold." Just then an alder bush drifted beneath them and bobbed downstream past potato fields and vegetable plots where one or two stooping figures were at work. It headed for the willow trees and bushes that hid the lower reaches of the river from view.

Katharina would have liked to wait until the alder bush was out of sight, but her brother's fear overruled her. "Scaredy-cat," she muttered as they walked on.

A horse suddenly whinnied so loudly that she jumped. It was being shod in the smithy beside the river. Kaspar, feeling more secure now, insisted on watching. The blacksmith, a broad-shouldered man in a leather apron, glanced at them with a smile on his flushed, sweating face. Beside him, holding the horse's bridle, stood the driver of the mail coach in his blue smock and straw hat. "Steady, Hassan, steady," he said to the animal. "I don't want you tipping any English tourists into the river come Sunday."

Kaspar asked why the man was hitting the horse on the foot, so Katharina told him that horses couldn't walk without shoes.

"How about it, children?" called the blacksmith, brandishing a steaming horseshoe in his tongs. "Shall I nail one

9

to your foot as well?" He grinned, and the driver bared his yellow teeth.

Panic-stricken, Kaspar ran off towards the high road with his sister in pursuit. Grown-ups were fond of making bad jokes – Katharina hated them for it. She'd often seen drunks in the taproom and in that state she believed them capable of anything, even nailing a horseshoe to a child's foot. Why not?

2

IF KATHARINA HAD BEEN ON HER WAY TO SCHOOL SHE would have turned left along the high road and into the village. But now she took the right-hand track, on which a heavily laden cart could be seen lumbering down the valley in the distance.

School had reopened only this week, after the long summer holidays. Schoolmaster Wyss taught forms one to four. Katharina was in form two. The third- and fourth-formers generally had classes in the mornings, the first- and second-formers in the afternoons except on Fridays, when the order was reversed. The only subjects the younger children shared with the older were local knowledge and singing, which fell on Tuesdays and Saturdays, because there was hardly room for all four forms in the schoolroom. Three pupils had to squeeze in behind a desk meant for two, and there were always a few children standing round the walls.

This morning Katharina had told Herr Wyss that she had to go to her grandmother's because of the baby, and that she would be back on Monday. Wyss had nodded and grunted his good wishes. He seemed quite uninterested in who did or did not come to school. Any pupil required to help at home could stay away as a matter of course. Attendance sometimes fell by half at haymaking time and when the second crop was cut. Katharina looked forward to those occasions in the hope that Herr Wyss would ask her plenty of questions. She got bored during lessons, which progressed far too slowly for her taste. All that a second-former had to know she had already mastered in the first form. She knew all her letters, could read any word, and had just as little trouble with her sums. In the first form you learnt how to add, in the second to subtract, in the third to multiply, and in the fourth to divide. Katharina failed to see why addition and subtraction could not be learnt at the same time. If two plus three made five, five minus three left two. Obvious.

Anna Elmer, who sat beside her, had failed to grasp this even though she was also a second-former. Pupils who shared a desk were sometimes told to ask each other questions. Anna had asked Katharina what five plus one was, and Katharina said six. Then Katharina asked Anna what six minus five was, and Anna didn't know the answer – in fact she lost her temper when Katharina told her and hissed that Katharina might have waited a bit longer for her to finish working it out. But Katharina found it incomprehensible that someone who knew that five plus one makes six wouldn't also know that six minus five leaves one. On another occasion Anna pulled her hair when she read out a word that Anna had failed to decipher. If she wouldn't accept help, thought Katharina, so be it: let her remain stupid.

Jakob had already taught Katharina how to multiply as well. Three times two children made six children. When the baby was born, they themselves would be six children: Anna and Regula, Jakob and herself, Kaspar and the baby. What if you divided six children by two children? Katharina wasn't quite sure how you divided children by children. You weren't taught that until the fourth form.

Hearing shouts, Katharina saw a group of children playing blind man's buff between the rifle association's clubhouse and the village fountain. She drew nearer and paused beside the road with Kaspar, watching. The players included Fridolin, the midwife's little boy; Burkhard, who was in Katharina's form; Anna, the girl who shared her desk at school; and Anna's younger brother and sister, Matthias and Gretli. Anna's elder brother, Oswald, a third-former, had tied the scarf round his head and was groping his way through the giggling children, who all came as close as possible, taunting him, then leapt back out of the way. "Here I am, Osi," cried Anna. "Can't you see me?" She sprang back as Oswald darted after her and swiftly hid behind Katharina, who was still standing at the roadside. Oswald blundered into Katharina and knocked her over. "Look out," she shouted angrily, but Anna only laughed. "Your turn now," said Oswald, removing the blindfold and holding it out. "I'm not playing," she said. She tried to wipe the mud off her cape, but it was so wet that she only made matters worse. "Too late," cried Burkhard, who proceeded to tie the scarf over her eyes from behind.

She tried to resist but the knot was too tight, and pulling the scarf off would have earned her slaps and punches. The boys were stronger than she was, especially Oswald, who was a year older. They took her by the hand, led her a little way off the road, spun her around a couple of times, and stepped back. At first she just stood there. She enjoyed playing blind man's buff as a rule, but now she wanted to get away as soon as possible. Her first few clumsy steps were greeted with derision – "Kathrine, latrine!" jeered Oswald – but she spun round and her outstretched hand struck her tormentor full in the face. Satisfied, she pulled off the blindfold, threw it at him and returned to the roadside, where Kaspar was waiting for her. Oswald made to follow but thought better of it and confined himself to sticking out his tongue at her. "Stop that silly noise," he told Burkhard, who was chuckling with glee. Then he tied the scarf round his head and the whole group backed away from him.

Katharina tried not to cry. Her sister Anna had got her black Sunday dress out of the chest for this visit to Granny, and now the hem that hung below the cape was dirty – thanks to Oswald and his sister. Osi should have been at school, but everyone knew he often played truant. His parents owned a big potato field, so he always pleaded that as an excuse, though Katharina had never seen him working there.

"Where are you going?" Anna called after her.

"To my Granny's," Katharina replied indignantly. She had already told Anna that morning, but if a girl couldn't count she probably couldn't keep anything else in her head either.

"Got you!" she heard Oswald shout. "No, you didn't," squeaked a little boy. She didn't turn round. Oswald liked playing with younger children because it made him the biggest. Yelling nasty things at a girl, that he could do. Katharina didn't care for Oswald.

"Did you get rid of the blindfold, then?" asked a man's voice.

"Yes," she said before she knew where it came from. Then she saw the old man sitting at his open window. He wore a thick cap with earflaps and was staring into space with milky eyes. It was Blind Meinrad. "Ah, yes, those naughty boys," he said, tittering to himself.

Fridolin came toddling over in floods of tears.

"What's wrong?" asked Katharina.

"Osi," he sobbed. "Mummy!" Then he ran off in the direction of a house nearby. Verena, the midwife with the red hair-ribbon, came out and bent over her weeping son. "What's the matter?" she asked, stroking his head, at which Fridolin unleashed a torrent of words, none of them intelligible.

Laughing, Verena produced a slice of dried pear from her apron and tried to shove it between the little boy's teeth, but he had to cry himself out first.

"Are you off to your grandmother's, Kathrin?" asked Verena.

Katharina nodded.

"I'll be going over to your mother soon," Verena went on, drying Fridolin's tears on a corner of her apron. "Are you looking forward to having a baby brother or sister?"

Katharina nodded again. "Yes," she said, though she wasn't really.

"It'll come tomorrow, I think," Verena said. "I'll be off to the Meur as soon as Peter comes home."

Katharina was glad to hear it. Still, she thought, Verena should have gone there at once. The way her mother had looked, lying there, she might need help already.

Fridolin was now chewing his slice of dried pear.

"How about you, Kaspar?" asked Verena. "Are you looking forward to the baby?"

"Want a little brother."

"Really?" said Verena. "What if you have a little sister?"

She gave him and Katharina a slice of pear each and advised them to hurry because it was going to rain again at any moment. Then she went indoors with Fridolin.

Katharina and Kaspar popped the slices of pear into their mouths.

"Why do you want a little brother?" asked Katharina.

"So I can hit him."

"Just wait – when he's big he'll hit you back."

"Won't."

"He will," said Katharina. "He'll give you a proper hiding."

It suddenly occurred to her that Kleophea lived in the same row, in the house next to last, and that the christening was the day after tomorrow. Kleophea was so young, she looked like an overgrown schoolgirl. How had she managed to have a child?

"Come on," said Katharina, "maybe we can see the baby."

They went to the window beside the front door. Katharina stood on tiptoe and peered through the rather misty window pane. Kleophea was sitting in the parlour with her blouse unbuttoned, suckling the baby. Her bulging breast protruded from the opening, and Katharina was surprised to see how big it was. When Kaspar clamoured to be allowed to look inside too, Kleophea glanced up and Katharina ran off, towing her brother behind her.

"What did you see?" he asked, when they were walking along the road.

"Only Kleophea," Katharina told him.

The rain started just as they reached the track that branched off towards the Bleiggen. Katharina put their hoods up, first Kaspar's, then her own. The track led straight up to a large house built into the hillside. Without knocking, Katharina opened the front door, beyond which lay a passage.

"Are we there yet?" asked Kaspar.

"No," Katharina told him, "this is the way through."

They walked along the gloomy passage, which smelt of dried mint and damp clothes, and Kaspar took care not to let go of his sister's hand. The passage was flanked by doors, all closed, beside which were hooks laden with hats and overcoats and stands full of walking sticks and umbrellas. Katharina and Kaspar climbed the stairs that led to the floor above, steep stairs with creaking treads. At the top they came to a landing with four doors leading off it, none of them open. An oleograph depicted Moses gazing heavenwards with a worried expression and two stone tablets in his hand. A woman's voice could be heard coming from behind one of the doors: "Seven whole days now, it's been raining."

"Yes, God help us," croaked a man's voice. "We'll be needing another Noah's Ark before we're done." A long bout of coughing followed.

Katharina and Kaspar quickly climbed the next flight of stairs and ran along the passage leading to the door at the rear of the building. A foul stench issued from the lavatory window that opened on to the passage. Emerging into the open air, the children were confronted by a flight of stone steps. Thereafter the track to the Bleiggen proceeded uphill as if nothing had interrupted it.

A gust of wind drove the rain into their faces. The door, which Katharina had tried to close with care, crashed shut.

"Want to wait here," said Kaspar, stopping dead.

"No," Katharina told him, "we must go on."

He started to cry.

"What's the point of waiting?" she demanded. "Yesterday it rained all day long."

The little boy peered up the mountainside through a veil of tears. It looked insuperable.

Katharina tried again. "We're sure to get some nice hot tea at Granny's," she said.

Kaspar sat down on the doorstep, raindrops mingling with the tears on his cheeks.

Katharina was at a loss. "All right," she said at length, "I'll go on alone." She turned and marched off up the slope, taking big strides. After a while she paused and looked back.

Kaspar was still sitting on the doorstep.

"Bye-bye!" Katharina called, waving to him. "I'll give your love to Granny." But Kaspar still didn't move.

18

Exasperated, she retraced her steps and planted herself in front of him.

"Well," she said. "are you coming or not?"

"Want to go home," said Kaspar.

A crash shook the air. He got to his feet, looking startled.

"Hear that?" said Katharina. "That's another lump of rock falling on our house."

He cast a fearful glance over his shoulder and took her hand. Slowly the two children climbed ever higher until the low-lying swaths of mist swallowed them up.

3

KATHARINA KNEW THE WAY, NOT THAT ONE COULD REALLY
miss it. The only turning came not far from their destination,
and that path led down to the church and the schoolhouse.
No matter how misty it was she would never have taken the
route to the village by mistake.

Kaspar had abandoned his resistance and was trotting
along beside her like a good boy, clinging to her hand.

Sounds filled the air: a big sound made by rain falling on
the leaves of trees that flanked their upward route, and a
lesser but more immediate sound of raindrops pattering on
their hoods and capes. Allied with the big sound was the roar
of the Sernf, which filled the whole valley; the lesser sound
included the scuffing of their shoes on the path, which was
strewn with small stones.

Katharina wondered, as she went, what her sister Regula
had meant by saying that Verena could haul a baby out of
its mother's tummy by the feet. It struck her that this was
yet another thing she didn't truly understand. Whenever
she tried to picture how a baby emerged from its mother's
tummy, she liked to imagine it sticking out one little arm to
begin with, so as to wave at the people who were awaiting
its arrival, and then perhaps the other, so that they could

haul it out. Papa sometimes gripped both her wrists with one hand and hoisted her into the air. To Katharina that seemed a practical position to be born in: with both hands extended arrow-like above the head, which needed special protection.

A baby could also stick its head or even its bottom out first, naturally, but each of those ways must surely be more painful for the mother than if it forged a path with its arms. Anyway, where was the opening in the tummy? All the apertures Katharina knew of were far too small for a whole baby. The likeliest place, she suspected, was the navel. She resolved to consult her elder sister on the subject when she got home.

Whatever the truth, it was an established fact that babies didn't usually come into the world feet first, but that Verena could cope even when they did. Mama would be all right, and so would the new baby, and from tomorrow onwards they would be three times two brothers and sisters, making six.

Kaspar came to a halt just short of a haystack. "Got to go," he said.

Katharina sighed. "Why didn't you go before we left?" she demanded, but he shook his head, obviously in dire straits, so she helped him to hitch up his cape and unbutton his flies. Before she could take her hands away, a yellow jet splashed her fingertips.

"Dirty little beast!" she cried, indignantly wiping her hands on the wet grass. "Be more careful, can't you?"

What a nuisance a younger brother could be! And now,

unless the baby turned out to be a girl, there was yet another one on the way. She hoped she wouldn't have to go off to the Bleiggen with *him* in four years' time, when the next baby arrived. She would send Kaspar instead, she thought grimly. Kaspar would then be four plus four makes eight, or a year older than she was now. It annoyed her to think that he would one day be older than her, even though she reflected that she herself would then be seven plus four makes eleven. What business did her little brother have, becoming older than her?

"Finished?" she asked, when he went on standing there with his willy in both hands, though no more wee-wee was coming out.

Kaspar nodded and stuffed it back into his trousers. Katharina did up his buttons and gave her hands another wipe on the grass.

"Ask sooner next time," she said reprovingly. He nodded with an abstracted air. It was only when she followed up her rebuke with another "Dirty little beast!" that he mumbled: "Not a dirty little beast."

"Yes, you are," she retorted. "You wee-weed over my hands."

"Didn't," he said.

That was the limit – flatly denying what he'd done only a minute ago. She grabbed his right hand, turned it over and slapped him on the palm the way Herr Wyss did in school, except that Herr Wyss used a ruler or a hazel switch.

Kaspar let out a yell. "Don't hit me!"

"Then don't tell lies," she said. "If you lie you get a slap, and that's that."

Kaspar remained unyielding. "I only did wee-wee on the grass."

Implacably, Katharina grabbed his left hand and gave him another slap, harder than the first.

Kaspar turned and ran back down the slope they'd just climbed.

Katharina sprinted after him in a fury. She caught up with him between two low walls and seized him by the hood. He tried to shake her off but she hung on tight, then tripped and fell over, bringing him down with her.

They scrambled to their feet in silence, both too startled to cry. It wasn't until Kaspar looked at his sister that he started to yell.

"You idiot," hissed Katharina. "You silly idiot."

But Kaspar was pointing at her face. "It's bleeding," he stammered.

Katharina felt her forehead, which was smarting, and there was blood on her fingers when she took them away. She'd grazed her head on one of the low walls.

She had to give her hands another wipe on the grass. "It's all your fault," she told him angrily. She felt her forehead again, and again her fingers came away bloody.

"T'isn't," he sobbed.

"Stay where you are," Katharina snapped at him. "I'm going for some dock leaves." She made for a clump of dock leaves, plucked some, and applied them to the cut.

"All right," she said, rejoining him. "Now we go to Granny's."

Clamping the cool leaves to her forehead, she took her

23

brother by the hand. Kaspar whimpered softly but abandoned himself to his fate, which was evidently to be dragged through a terrible rainstorm by his elder sister – dragged, moreover, to his grandmother, who lived a long, long way from home. At home a new baby sister was being born, and at home lumps of rock were tumbling down the mountainside. Kaspar hoped with all his heart that they would crush his new baby sister to death, then everything would be the way it had always been.

They were past the haystack when they heard someone yodel in the distance.

Katharina came to a halt. "Did you hear?" she said to Kaspar. "That's Granny, she's calling us. Come on, let's call back."

She drew a deep breath and gave a long, drawn-out cry that ended in a dying fall, the kind their mother always gave when summoning them from the kitchen window. No sooner had the echoes faded than their grandmother responded in kind.

Katharina smiled. "You see? She's heard us," she said to Kaspar, who was standing there, uncomprehending, in the damp mist. "Why didn't you call too?"

"Where's Granny?" he asked.

"Up there," said Katharina.

Kaspar couldn't see any Granny. All he could see was an impossibly steep track that traversed a field before disappearing into some gloomy trees so tall that their tops were in the clouds.

"Come on," said his sister. "We'll soon be there."

Kaspar had no choice but to believe her. He took her hand again. It felt like a pebble from the river bed, wet and cold.

Just before they reached the trees a shaft of lightning lit up the murky afternoon sky. It was so bright that both children screwed up their eyes. Almost simultaneously, a thunderclap made the air shudder as if an avalanche were bearing down on them from the Bleiggen.

Kaspar started crying again. Katharina quickened her steps, towing him behind her. "No need to be scared," she told him, "it's only a thunderstorm."

She herself was trembling with fear. Only last year, Afra Bäbler from the fourth form had been killed by lightning while looking for her goat on the Falzüber Alp. The men who brought her down to the valley on a sledge had stopped off at the Meur for a drink. Afra remained outside, lashed to the sledge and wrapped in a blanket so you couldn't see her face. At the funeral the whole school had gathered round the grave and sung "Rosine went into the garden and picked three flowers", the song whose third verse told how Jesus welcomed Rosine, took her up to heaven with him, and wrote her parents a letter telling them how happy she was to live in such a beautiful place. But Katharina hadn't been able to sing because she couldn't help crying and didn't understand how anyone could sing when someone had died; and children shouldn't have to die in any case.

They reached the edge of the trees and came to a halt, breathing hard. Katharina could hear a cowbell tinkling, but where was the cow?

"We'll wait here," she said.

"Want to go home," said Kaspar.

"Don't be silly!"

"I'm frightened."

"Silly boy, it isn't far now."

How glad she was to have someone to take care of. On her own she would have been beside herself with terror.

The clouds were split by a second flash of lightning that lingered in the sky. It cleft the valley in two and zigzagged into the Sernf. The thunder was so deafening, it seemed to come from both sides of the valley at once.

Kaspar continued to weep.

Intent on scolding him, Katharina ran through a mental list of the direst expressions she could use for the purpose, from cry-baby to sissy to piddle-pants, but she suddenly changed her mind. She sat down beside him on a tree trunk and said: "Come on, I'll tell you a story."

And while shafts of lightning threaded the sky like sinister spiders' webs and successive claps of thunder rolled down the valley, she told her little brother the story of the Great Flood, which she had heard last week in Sunday school: how God had ceased to take pleasure in human beings because they were so sinful; and how he had resolved to make it rain for so long that everyone drowned, but regretted his decision a little and warned Noah in time and commanded him to build a big ship called the Ark, and to take two of every kind of animal on board with him, as well as his wife and his three sons and their wives; and how the windows of heaven had opened and it rained for 40 days and nights until everyone drowned – human beings and

26

animals alike – and Noah alone was saved together with his family and all the animals in his Ark, which floated on the waters.

And Kaspar stopped crying and listened to his sister, whose descriptions became more and more elaborate the longer the thunderstorm lasted. She told him how a lake came up the valley from Glarus and began to submerge everything, first Engi and Matt and then Elm, and how the marmots crept out of their burrows and fled into the Alps with the chamois and the mountain goats, making for the Martinsloch, until in the end they were all standing on the very crests and the marmots whistled loudly before the big lake washed over them and swallowed them up.

"What about the fish?" asked Kaspar, when she described how all the animals had drowned.

Katharina was disconcerted by this question. Parson Mohr hadn't said anything about it.

"Oh, them," she said airily. "God liked the fish, so they didn't drown. Besides, they could swim."

She was dissatisfied with this explanation. Why should God be fonder of fish than of marmots? She really ought to ask the parson, but the others would be bound to laugh at her.

When she got to the bit where the Ark was floating on the great waters with Noah and all the surviving animals on board, she fell silent.

"What happened then?" asked Kaspar.

"I don't know," she said. "That's as far as the parson got. On Sunday he'll tell us how it goes on."

All at once, their grandmother loomed up in front of them under a black umbrella.

"What happened, child?" she asked when she saw Katharina's grazed forehead.

Nothing, said Katharina: she'd simply slipped on the wet track and fallen over. Looking up, she saw a cow on the hillside and, right at the top, the house. Then Granny took her hand, and Katharina took Kaspar's hand and, sheltering beneath the huge umbrella, they set off up the steep, grassy slope while the receding thunderstorm rumbled away down the valley.

4

THEY SAT AT THE KITCHEN TABLE: GRANNY, KATHARINA
and Kaspar. The two children each had a bowl of steaming
herb tea and a slice of pear cake in front of them. Katharina
had nearly finished hers; Kaspar was still chewing the only
mouthful he'd taken.

They were both so wet that Granny had changed all
their clothes. Her cupboards still contained some children's
garments that might have been waiting there for years, just
for the benefit of grandchildren who got soaked to the
skin. She was delighted to find they fitted. Katharina put
on a blue dress that smelt of lavender and, over it, a grey
knitted jacket. The shirt for Kaspar was a little on the large
side, being one that his father had worn until he went to
school.

"You look almost like my Schaaggli, sitting there," said
Granny, having rolled up Kaspar's sleeves a little.

Papa's real name was Jakob, so why, Katharina wondered,
did she never hear it used? Mama called him Ätti; so did
Katharina and her brothers and sisters. The men from the
village called him Joggli or Meurjoggli, and Granny referred
to him as Schaaggli. Once she had heard her mother call
him "my little goat", or not so much call as murmur, when

they had come upstairs from the taproom one night and Katharina was standing outside the door because she couldn't sleep. No one would ever have guessed that his name was Jakob. No one ever called her Katharina, either. The others addressed her as Kathrine or Kathrinli, and the longer she heard the latter the less she liked it. Why "little" Kathrin? Wasn't she a second-former already? Wasn't she asked to do things that would normally have been expected of a grown-up? When was the last time her big sister Anna had trudged up to the Bleiggen during a thunder-storm with a younger brother in tow, like a nurse-maid? She preferred it when Mama or Granny called her Didi. It was almost like another name, not that she knew where it came from.

But she was really called Katharina and she was proud of having such a nice long name, which she had written on the slate she took to school with her. When she was a grown woman she would insist on being addressed as Katharina, and if someone came and tried to kiss her behind the house, the way Hans-Kaspar did with Anna, she would tell him: "Only if you call me Katharina."

"And how's Kathrin?" Granny asked.

Katharina gave a little start and thought for a moment. Kathrin was her mother.

"She sends her love," she replied, "and so does Anna."

"But how is she?" Granny asked again.

"Not too well," Katharina said hesitantly. "She's in bed. She keeps puffing and blowing – she can't help it."

"Who's looking after her?"

Katharina told her that Regula had sent for Verena the midwife, and that she would be going to the Meur that evening.

"God be praised," said Granny. "Let's hope it'll soon be over, then she can get up and go back to work." Abruptly she turned to Kaspar and asked: "Are you looking forward to having another little brother or sister?"

Kaspar nodded warily. It hadn't escaped him that this question harboured a lurking danger.

"Kaspar wants a little brother," said Katharina.

"And you?"

"I'd sooner have a sister."

Granny got up and went over to the kitchen door. "Did you hear?" she shouted up the stairs. "The midwife will be with Kathrin before the day's out!"

From upstairs came the plaintive cries of a baby, promptly followed by a woman's soothing voice. The baby stopped crying at once. "She drinks like a calf!" called the voice, then all was silent again. Granny shut the door. Wood crackled in the stove. There was a crash somewhere in the distance.

Kaspar stopped chewing. Tears began to roll down his cheeks.

"You mustn't be frightened, little one," said Granny, stroking his hair. "The thunderstorm's over."

Unmoved by this, Kaspar continued to cry.

"You're here now," Granny went on. "Eat up your nice pear cake and drink up your tea."

But the little boy was beset by another fear altogether. It

welled up inside him like the flood in the valley, submerging his tea and pear cake.

"What's the matter?" asked his grandmother. "Come on, tell Granny."

Kaspar shook his head. He didn't want to say anything, not a word.

Granny turned to Katharina. "Do *you* know what's the matter with him?"

Katharina shrugged. "He'll stop in a minute."

But Kaspar went on crying. He was listening to his grandmother and his sister and could understand what they said. But it was as if they were standing outside the front door, and inside, where he was sitting, he had a second pair of ears and could hear his sister saying: "That's another lump of rock falling on our house." And the bowl and the pear cake and the table went blurred before his eyes, but he also had a second pair of eyes. And those eyes, which he had long since opened, showed him a huge rock bearing down on the house in which he lived and smashing everything he was fond of: not only the bed he slept in with Katharina and Jakob, and the rocking horse he squabbled over with Katharina, but Züsi the cat as well; and (here Kaspar shut his second pair of eyes, but he could see with them just the same) the lump of rock was big enough to crush Papa and Mama and Jakob and Regula and Anna, and all he could see was one of Papa's shoes and one of Anna's arms peeping out of the ruins of their home. And he was expected to drink tea and eat pear cake?

"He's gone to sleep," said Granny.

Katharina glanced at her brother. His head had subsided on to the pear cake as if it were a pillow. The sweet brown pear jam was beginning to ooze out and creep from his cheek into his hair. She went to pick up his head by the hair and pull the plate away, but her grandmother caught hold of her hand.

"Leave him be," she said quietly. "It was a long walk for him."

Then she stood up and said: "Come along, you can help me put him to bed. I'll carry him upstairs." Bending down, she put her right arm under the sleeping boy's legs and her left arm under his shoulders and gently lifted him off the kitchen bench.

Katharina had already got up and opened the door to the hallway, which was cold enough to give her the shivers.

Granny emerged from the kitchen. Katharina shut the door behind them and followed her to the stairs. As she did so, she brushed one of the two wet capes with her shoulder and shrank away. It felt as if someone were reaching for her, or as if she'd been touched by some unfamiliar animal.

She kept close behind her grandmother, whose weight made the stairs creak. When she herself trod on the same stair she heard nothing. She was too little to make stairs creak. That would change one day, she thought. One day every staircase she climbed and every house she entered would creak loudly – yes, houses would creak if she as much as walked up to them. No wet cape would dare to touch her. Then everyone would call her Katharina and take her seriously.

"Is Didi asleep?" asked the woman's voice through a half-open door.

They had reached the first floor.

"No, it's Kaspar," Granny replied. "Would you open the door for me, Kathrin?" she asked, jerking her head at the door beyond the one from which the woman's voice had come.

Katharina squeezed past her and opened it. The bedroom beyond was almost colder than the stairwell. All it contained, apart from a wardrobe, was a big bed with a broad quilt and two pillows.

"Turn back the bedclothes," said Granny, still in the same low voice, as if they were sharing a secret.

Katharina did as she was told. Her grandmother laid Kaspar down on the sheet and peeled off his trousers.

"Our nightshirts are still downstairs," said Katharina.

"Never mind," said Granny, "he can sleep in his shirt."

She covered Kaspar up, and the sight of him asleep suddenly made Katharina look forward to bed. The bed here was bigger than hers at home, or perhaps it seemed so only because she had to share hers with Regula and Jakob as well as her little brother. She went to the window and looked out, but the sky was so overcast that all she could see were the trees nearest the house. Beyond them was an expanse of grey nothingness.

Katharina was rather proud of having brought her brother up here alone, the way Elmer, the mountain guide, had done with his English tourists on the Hausstock. Not long ago Elmer had boasted in the taproom of having climbed the Hausstock with two Englishmen. He said he'd told them to wait for better weather or they wouldn't see a thing, but they'd insisted on going so they went, and sure enough they hadn't seen a thing. It was so misty that he himself had almost lost his way on the Meer Glacier.

"Come, Kathrinli," Granny said softly. She was already standing by the door with her hand on the latch.

Katharina walked past her and paused outside the first door, which was ajar.

"Hello, Didi," said the woman seated on the edge of the bed, suckling her baby.

"Hello, Margret," Katharina murmured, staring at the woman's breast. The baby was sucking away with its eyes wide open. It was definitely bigger than Kleophea's baby and Margret's breast was even bigger than Kleophea's – and that had been pretty big.

Margret lived here at Granny's. Her husband was Katharina's uncle. But only Katharina called him Uncle Paul; to the other children he was plain Paul. Two more uncles, Johannes and Fridolin, also lived in the house. People were uncles and aunts if your father or mother was their brother or sister. Katharina wasn't entirely sure what that made Margret, who sat looking up at her and said: "Brave girl, coming all this way through the storm."

A smile appeared on Katharina's face.

"Yes, there hasn't been such a thunderstorm for many a long day," Margret added. The baby loudly smacked its lips as she squeezed her breast between her thumb and forefinger. "Weren't you frightened?"

Katharina didn't care for that question. Of course she'd been frightened. If it hadn't been for little Kaspar, who had needed her protection and was far more frightened still, she would have died of fear.

But as a rule anyone who admitted to being frightened was scoffed at. Coward was one of the worst terms of abuse that could be used between children – or grown-ups, for that matter. Gutlessness – wasn't that what Beat Rhyner had been accused of in the taproom last night by Elmer, the mountain guide and midwife's husband? Beat had jumped up and told Elmer that the chamois he shot had more brains than he did. It was years since they'd remained at such an altitude at this time of year, so why didn't he ask *them* if they were gutless?

The men had been arguing about the slabs of rock that kept breaking off and falling down the mountainside, and whether they signified anything or not.

Katharina was well acquainted with Beat Rhyner, who lived at the back of the Meur. A head taller than her father, he was a forester and certainly no coward. But Beat hadn't admitted to being frightened; he'd blamed it all on the chamois. He and his wife Barbara had five children, the same as Papa and Mama, but soon, when Mama had her sixth, they wouldn't have as many any longer. Perhaps the Rhyners would also have another child – you never could tell – and then both families would have the same number of children once more. Katharina hoped the mid-wife was there by now.

"Weren't you frightened?" Margret repeated. Her baby had

stopped feeding and was lying in her arms with its eyes closed.

Katharina raised her head, looked at the woman with the sleeping infant, and said: "Yes, I was."

5

"THEY'LL SOON BE DRY," SAID GRANNY.

She had draped the children's nightshirts and under-clothes over the pole above the big slate stove in the parlour. Katharina had discovered, on opening the bundle, that every-thing inside it was sodden. She deposited her wooden doll, Lisi, on the sofa beside the stove. "You can get warm there," she told her, with an enquiring glance at her grandmother.

The thing was, Papa thought children of school age shouldn't play with dolls any longer. That was why she always had to make sure he wasn't around when she brought Lisi out, and it was as well to ask Mama if she was expecting him home soon. Katharina couldn't understand this. Lisi had always been her favourite toy and she liked playing with her most of all when school had been boring. She often sat the doll on a piece of firewood instead of a school bench and played Schoolmaster Wyss, and Lisi would begin by being even more of a dunce than Anna Elmer and not even know the answer to one plus one. But when the teacher advanced on her menacingly and brandished a little hazel twig under her nose she suddenly knew everything and became even cleverer than the teacher himself, juggling with numbers bigger than a thousand as easy as pie.

When her grandmother uttered no word of criticism and actually commended her for taking such good care of her doll, Katharina realized that no paternal homecoming need be feared in this house. Grandfather was dead, after all. He'd died of a goitre – however you died of a goitre – and Uncle Paul, who was bound to be home soon, was a good-natured man who enjoyed fun and games and surely wouldn't object if a wooden doll sat on the sofa beside the stove. Actually, Papa was also good-natured and enjoyed fun and games. He used to toss her into the air and catch her; or she'd stand with her back to him, bend down and put her hands between her legs, and he'd grip them and pull, lifting her at the same time, with the result that she turned a somersault and didn't know for a moment which way up she was. Then he would set her down in front of him and say: "There, *that* cheese is turned." But he hadn't done that for a long time, worse luck. Ever since Kaspar had discovered the somersault game, Papa only played it with him.

Kaspar was Papa's favourite in general, or so it seemed to Katharina. The little boy had only to pester him long enough and he'd get a slice of pear, but Papa never gave her one, not these days. Recently, when he'd caught her elder brother Jakob filching some slices of dried pear from the storeroom, he put him over his knee and smacked his bottom. Jakob burst into tears and demanded to know why Kaspar could have slices of pear when he couldn't, but Papa's only response had been to tell him to hold his tongue or he'd get another walloping.

Appalled by such scenes, Katharina would take refuge in

the children's communal bedroom but leave the door open so as not to miss anything. It struck her that grown-ups enjoyed hitting children when they couldn't think of anything better to do. Hadn't Jakob been right to ask that question about Kaspar, and hadn't he been right to try to get the same as him? No, apparently not. Life was like that: grown-ups could decide what was right and what wasn't, and they could also call something right when it wasn't right at all. If you were a child and wanted to be in the right, it usually ended in tears.

Mama was less to be feared. But although she didn't often pull their hair or tweak their earlobes, she took just as little trouble to find out who was in the right. If two of them got into an argument she simply grabbed them both by the ear or knocked their heads together and said: "That'll teach you to squabble."

Katharina felt convinced that she herself would be quite different when she grew up. She intended to be just – just but merciful like the Emperor of China in the school primer, who sentenced an official found guilty of theft to have both his hands chopped off. The official's daughter came to the Emperor, went down on her knees before him, and held out her own hands to be chopped off instead of her father's. The Emperor was so touched by this, he let the father off. Regula had read that story aloud to Katharina from her primer. Titled "The heathen girl who loved her father more than herself", it made such a deep impression on Katharina that she wanted to read it herself again and again. Regula had eventually taken the book away. Katharina would come to it in the fifth form, she said, and that was soon enough.

"What are you thinking about, child?" asked Granny, who was standing by the parlour door. Katharina was still sitting beside her doll on the sofa.

"Do *we* chop people's hands off when they steal things?" she asked.

"What on earth gave you that idea, Didi?" Granny looked shocked. "Where would they do such a thing?"

"In China," said Katharina. "The heathens do it. It says so in Regula's school book."

"Exactly," said Granny. "The heathens may do it but we don't. With us, people who steal go to prison. That's bad enough."

A dog barked outside.

"That'll be Paul," Granny said. "He went to the upper pasture with Nero."

Katharina got up and went through the kitchen to the hallway. She wanted to see the dog. By the time she reached the front door her uncle was chaining his black sheepdog to the kennel. The wet animal shook itself so vigorously that drops of water flew in all directions.

"Wait, can't you?" Paul said with a laugh. Then he caught sight of Katharina. "Look," he said to Nero, "there's Didi. Go on, go for her!"

Nero started barking and Katharina quickly retreated a step. This was another grown-up's joke – one that Paul found funny but she didn't.

"He won't eat you," said Paul. "Well," he added, almost

in the same breath, "have you brought some fine weather with you?"

Katharina didn't know what she was supposed to say.

"Hello, Uncle Paul," she said softly, and went back to her grandmother in the kitchen.

She would have liked to pat Nero, but now she didn't dare. Uncle Paul had set the dog on her, after all, and she couldn't be sure it remembered her from her last visit. They had no dog at the Meur. They used to have one, Mama had told her one day, but it kept growling at the customers in the taproom, so they'd been compelled to shoot it and didn't want another. A pity, thought Katharina. She did have Züsi the cat, admittedly, and you could fondle her too, but a cat wasn't the same as a dog. A cat would never accompany you to the upper pasture. With Züsi, you would think yourself lucky if you saw her now and then at mealtimes; the rest of the day she did as she pleased. Katharina also disliked her habit of catching mice, though Papa said that that was what she was there for. Once when Züsi was playing with a mouse on the forecourt, catching it and then letting it run for a bit, Katharina had managed to rescue the mouse by grabbing the cat and bearing her off. Züsi not only resisted but became so enraged that she scratched Katharina's cheek and drew blood. Meanwhile, the mouse had scampered under the bench beside the front door and disappeared. It left a tiny trail of blood behind, but at least it escaped with its life. Katharina could still remember how it had stung when Mama trickled some tincture of arnica on to the scratch, and how it had also stung when Papa scolded her. "That's what she's there for," he'd said again, adding after a moment's pause: "You little dunce!"

She also had a distinct recollection of the sidelong glance Mama had given her when she showed Papa two withered lettuce leaves from the vegetable garden and said: "The mice have been at the roots."

That had happened in the days before she went to school. Since then she'd been careful not to interfere with Züsi whenever she did what she was there for. Sometimes, though, during bedtime prayers, when Mama broke off for a moment to let them pray for other people and Katharina couldn't think of anyone in particular, she remembered the tiny drops of blood on the flagstones and prayed that the mouse would never be caught.

She liked to stroke Züsi, for all that, and it was nice when the cat purred contentedly and arched her back a little. Why didn't people stroke each other that way? Or did they only do so in secret, behind the house at nightfall, when they called each other "my little goat"?

Uncle Paul was now in the hall. "How's the baby, Margret?" he called up the stairs. "Ssh!" came Margret's voice from above. The stairs creaked softly. "She's asleep," she told her husband, following him into the kitchen.

"Foul weather," said Paul. He shook his head almost like Nero. "You get soaked to the skin."

Granny poured him and Margret some herb tea out of her big teapot, and they both sat down at the kitchen table and started discussing whether or not to cut the second crop of hay. Granny listed all the neighbours who had already done so, but Paul said their hay was so damp it would rot in the stack, and he preferred to wait for at least one sunny day. St Peter would surely manage that in the end, though what had got into him? It was ages since they'd had a thunderstorm like today's. "You nearly had to swim up the mountain, eh, Didi?" he said, smiling at her.

Katharina nodded and said nothing. Swim up the mountain . . . another grown-up's joke. She couldn't swim in any case – none of the village children could. In summer, when it was hot, the boys sometimes created a little pool by damming the Raminer with stones and lay down in the cold water in their underpants, but that was no pastime for a girl. Katharina liked to sit on the banks of the stream and dabble her feet in it until they were icy cold. Then she sunned them until they were warm right through. Getting cold was nice if you could warm up again afterwards. She hoped Lisi was dry by now. Why didn't Paul get changed? she wondered. His pale blue shirt was so wet, it was dark blue across the shoulders and up to the elbows. Granny was Paul's mother, so why didn't she say something about it? Or was she Margret's mother? When they came in today, she and Kaspar, Granny had produced some dry clothes before they could even sit down at the table. But Uncle Paul was a grown-up and so was Margret. Granny couldn't order them around any more.

"I went to fetch the pair of them," she said. "They got to the foot of the lower pasture just when the thunderstorm was at its worst."

"The pair of them?" said Paul. Had Regula or Jakob come

too? No, Granny told him, only Kaspar. The little ones always gave the most trouble when a baby was on the way. Kaspar had been so tired he'd fallen asleep at the kitchen table.

"What do you think of the weather, Kathrinli?" Paul asked suddenly.

Katharina was unprepared for this question. She'd just been reflecting that when the baby was born she would no longer be classed with the little ones, so the sooner it was born the better. Kaspar would be surprised how quickly the new child would turn into Papa's pet instead of him. Strangely enough, the little ones were not only the biggest nuisance but the biggest favourites.

"Eh?" said her uncle, and gave her a cheerful wink.

Katharina was annoyed. What did he mean? Was it another joke? What did she think of the weather? The same as everyone: it was awful. She too would have preferred the sun to come out. She drew a deep breath and said, "Maybe the Great Flood will come soon."

The three grown-ups stared at her in surprise.

6

KATHARINA WAS SITTING BESIDE MARGRET AT THE FOOT of the long kitchen table – or was it at the head? – listening to her uncles arguing.

They were seated facing her. Paul was the eldest but also the shortest of them all; he was even a little shorter than his young wife, as Katharina had noticed when they entered the kitchen together. Paul had curly hair and sly, humorous eyes. He spoke fast, and Katharina had the same slight mistrust of him as she had of anyone who was fond of telling jokes. People who told jokes didn't say what they meant and Katharina was always afraid that Paul *did* mean what he said. How was she supposed to tell at once whether a blacksmith intended to nail a horseshoe to her foot or an uncle to set his dog on her?

Johannes, on the other hand, was a tall, thoughtful, good-humoured man. He spoke more slowly than Paul, and she was sure he meant what he said. His hair was curly too, but he had a broader face and a big nose, and his lips were always parted a little, even when he wasn't speaking.

Fridolin was the only one of the three who had a moustache. It was odd that he, too, should have curly hair, because Granny's hair was quite straight. She combed it back and braided it into a plait which lay coiled on the back of her head like a snake. Katharina didn't know how old her grandmother was; she only knew that she had a lot of sons and daughters – many more than her parents. By rights, a woman of her age should have gone grey long ago, like old Elsbeth who lived next door to the Meur, but Granny's snakelike plait was thick and brown and, although her skin was rather wrinkled, her face was the colour of fresh pear cake.

Fridolin always spoke with his head tilted back a little, as if looking up at the mountains. He had just described how he'd earned a day's pay although the slate quarry where he worked had been closed the day before because of the danger of rockfalls. He had helped the owners of the Martinsloch, the inn immediately below the Plattenberg, to load their belongings on to a wagon and transport them to relatives who lived in Matt. Chests, trunks, beds, tables, chairs – all had been stored in a barn "until the worst is over", as Fridolin put it.

They must be out of their minds, Paul declared. The worst was over long ago, and only an idiot would close an inn because of a few stones. Now anyone who wanted a drink would go to the Meur instead. "So much the better for your papa, eh, Didi? He's no coward – he wouldn't go scurrying off to Matt when the mountains make a bit of noise, would he?"

Katharina merely nodded. Coward . . . another mention of the word she disliked. Were you really a coward if you didn't fancy getting crushed by a rock? If you didn't want to be a coward, what did that make you instead? She couldn't think of an appropriate term for someone who deliberately stood beneath a crag from which slabs of rock were falling.

Fridolin told Paul he had it precisely the wrong way round: the innkeeper and his family would have been crazy to stay. Only two days ago a rockfall from the Gelber Kopf had buried half the Rütiweid, so much so that the district councillors had gone up to inspect it, and yesterday at five there'd been such a crash you'd have thought General Suvorov was bombarding the French with his heaviest artillery, and what came bouncing down the mountainside had smashed half the slate warehouse, and it was a mercy that none of them had been hit, and a boulder had come to rest just behind the Martinsloch, shattering the window panes and dislodging the antlers on the walls, and the next might easily land on the roof. And there were plenty more where that one had come from.

Johannes turned to Fridolin and asked why he went on working at the quarry if it was so dangerous.

"Where else am I to work?" demanded Fridolin, looking up at his own and his brothers' shadows, which the tallow candles were projecting on the kitchen wall like a mountain range. "Four and a half francs a day," he went on. "Where else would I earn as much – at your joiner's workshop?"

Paul said that Fridolin wouldn't earn a thing as long as the district council couldn't think of anything better to do than close the slate quarry.

The councillors knew what they were doing, Fridolin said. Tomorrow a committee would be going up the mountainside to assess the situation.

48

"A committee?" scoffed Paul. "Who'll be on it?"

Fridolin said he'd heard that Elmer, the mountain guide, would be going.

"Peter Elmer?" asked Johannes, looking surprised.

"No, Heiri. And a district councillor. And someone from the canton as well, I expect."

"From the canton, eh?" said Paul. "And who would that be?"

Fridolin didn't know, and for a moment they all fell silent, staring at their mugs, the cheese rind on their plates, and the empty dishes that had once held boiled potatoes.

"Forester Seeli," said Katharina.

All heads turned in her direction. The mountain range on the wall swayed and the peaks canted sideways as if on the point of collapse.

"Who told you that, child?" asked Granny.

Beat Rhyner, the forester, had mentioned the name to her father in the taproom that morning, and Katharina had laughed until Papa reprimanded her. Seeli: Little Lake. Unable to conceive that anyone could bear such a name, let alone a forester, Katharina had pictured a miniature lake roaming the woods and creeping through the trees.

She couldn't suppress another little chuckle before telling the tilted heads where she'd heard the name.

"Well, well, fancy that," said Paul. He gave her a nod, then turned to his youngest brother and said that if Seeli and Co. took it into their heads to close the slate works he could help him bring in the second crop of hay.

Fridolin promptly asked how much Paul would pay him.

49

A quarter, said Paul. "A quarter litre of wine?" Fridolin retorted. "You must be joking." No, said Paul, a quarter of a quarryman's pay – that was all he could afford. Fridolin was one of the family, after all; he lived on the premises and paid Mother for his board.

And so it went on, back and forth, until Johannes put his hand on Fridolin's shoulder and said he could come and work at the joiner's shop. They could use an extra pair of hands and he thought they could manage to pay half a quarryman's wage, or two francs at least.

Katharina suspected that two francs didn't quite amount to half the said wage. She thought: If two buns cost four centimes, what does one bun cost? It was that kind of sum, and in the case of four and a half francs you had to divide the half by two, but that was still beyond her.

Paul asked why they suddenly needed an extra pair of hands. Were they repanelling Zentner's house?

No, Johannes said, it was something else.

"What?" asked Fridolin.

"Coffins," Johannes replied.

His employer had discovered that they were running low, and they always had to have a few of every size in stock because you never knew when the next one would be needed. Last week they'd got rid of two infants' coffins at a stroke when Louise Elmer's twins had died in quick succession, and now they were clean out of coffins for babies – not to mention fatties or beanpoles, he added with a slow grin.

Paul burst out laughing and Fridolin smiled in an abstracted way, but Granny shook her head disapprovingly and Margret said: "Really, Johannes!"

Katharina didn't join in the laughter. The words "infants' coffins" had jolted her and summoned up a vision of Afra Bäbler's grave. An infant's coffin must be half the size of a child's at most, she reflected. How long would it be, an infant's coffin? She tried to work it out in feet and inches, and all at once she was back in the bedroom at home, listening to her mother's laboured breathing. What if the baby died at birth? Would Johannes have to make it a little coffin with Fridolin's assistance? She resolved to pray at bedtime, really hard, that the baby would be born hale and hearty, so that it could grow up with them and not need a little coffin and be strong enough to climb to the Bleiggen with Kaspar when the next baby arrived.

She heard Nero bark and rattle his chain. A man spoke to him quietly and he fell silent. There was a knock, the front door opened, and the man called: "It's me!"

"Come in," Granny said, without getting up. She seemed to know who "me" was.

The kitchen door opened and a young man stood there, almost filling the doorway and casting a giant shadow on the ceiling. Katharina now recognised him too. It was Hans-Kaspar, who had kissed her sister behind the Meur that night. He lived next door to her grandmother.

"Sit down," said Granny. She and Margret, who were sitting side by side, shuffled closer to Katharina.

Hans-Kaspar sat down beside the old woman, who poured him a mug of tea. "Anyone else?" she asked. Katharina pushed her mug into the middle of the table and her grandmother refilled it. At home the children never got more than one mug. Granny took Margret's mug too and refilled it. "Drink up, Margret," she said, handing it back, "so the baby doesn't go thirsty."

Paul got up and went over to the small cupboard beside the stove. Producing a bottle and four little glasses, he put them down on the table, opened the bottle and filled the glasses. Katharina's nostrils were tickled by a pungent smell she both liked and loathed. She liked it because it had a strange smell of herbs and she loathed it because the menfolk usually drank too much, becoming loud-mouthed and bad-tempered.

The four men raised their glasses and took a swallow.

"What news?" Granny asked.

"I've just come from the Meur," Hans-Kaspar told her. "Everyone sends their regards. The midwife's with Kathrin. She'll be staying overnight – the baby may arrive any time now, she says."

"A good thing she's there," said Granny. "Eh, Margret?"

Margret nodded. Six months ago the midwife had got to her too late because it all happened so quickly. By the time Verena reached Granny's house little Anna was already there, and her grandmother had helped with the bearing down and the delivery and the umbilical cord, the blood and the hot water, as if she'd been doing it all her life.

"We'll pray for her tonight," Granny commanded, looking around the table. No one spoke for a moment or two. Katharina was shocked to realise that she herself had been meaning to pray for the baby alone, but Mama, of course, was just as important – far more so, in fact. It would be worse if something happened to Mama than if it happened to the baby, who was still a total stranger.

"You were the only one Anna sent her regards to, I suppose?" said Paul. The three uncles gave a meaningful laugh. Katharina thought she saw Hans-Kaspar blush. He didn't answer the question – just said he'd looked in at the Gasthof Elmer and heard that a committee was going up the Plattenberg tomorrow. Did they know who would be on it?

"Forester Seeli," everyone chorused.

Hans-Kaspar looked taken aback. "Who told you?"

Paul jerked his head at Katharina and said: "Our eldest."

More laughter filled the room and the shadowy mountain range on the wall wavered. At last a grown-up's joke that Katharina could grasp at once: she was the youngest person at the table, of course, not the eldest. She quickly joined in, giggling audibly, and the men took another pull at their glasses.

Hans-Kaspar seemed rather disappointed.

"Who else is going?" Paul asked him.

"Heiri Elmer the guide, Councillor Samuel Freitag, and District Forester Marti."

"What?" exclaimed Paul. "Marti comes from Matt. We don't need anyone from Matt telling us Elmers what to do."

"All these foresters," muttered Fridolin. "Let's hope they know something about rockfalls as well."

"There are piles of trees up there," said Johannes. "They're lying all over the place. You can see them from here. If only someone would bring them down, there'd be coffins enough for the whole village."

"You and your coffins," Granny said. "Let's talk about something more cheerful."

"All right," Paul suggested, "let's talk about the cantonal forester." He turned to Hans-Kaspar. "Is he there already?"

"Yes, he arrived an hour ago. He's staying at the Gasthof Elmer."

"Well," said Fridolin, "things must be serious, then. I suppose it means the slate works will be closed again tomorrow?"

"Yes," said Hans-Kaspar. "That's just what I was going to tell you."

Fridolin scratched his moustache. "In that case," he said to Johannes, "I'll come and help you with your coffins."

7

KATHARINA SHIVERED WITH COLD AND FEAR AS SHE MADE her way to the stairs from the lavatory, which was situated at the back of the hall. As soon as you raised the heavy lid, disgusting smells rose like evil spirits emerging from a dark dungeon. Usually the edge of the hole was still damp, or had even been soiled by the last person to sit on it, and you had to wipe it with the little cloth that lay alongside, which wasn't too clean itself as a rule. Things were even worse at home because the taproom customers used the same lavatory as the rest of the family and the Rhyners, and Katharina could still remember, only too vividly, how she had once done it in her knickers when someone went on sitting there too long. You must always wash your hands in the fountain afterwards, Schoolmaster Wyss had impressed on them, but that applied to only one of the two calls of nature – the one the family referred to as a "Fat Aunt". Katharina was now doing a "Thin Aunt", but she was terribly afraid of standing up too soon and weeing on the edge of the hole. Having failed in the darkness to find any little cloth to wipe the wood with, she swiftly replaced the lid over the hole to imprison the evil-smelling spirits and darted out into the hall.

Men's loud voices were issuing from the half-open kitchen

door, and the glow that escaped through the crack overlay the floorboards like a luminous carpet, lighting up the steep flight of stairs to the floor above.

As she climbed the stairs Katharina heard them creak beneath her, very softly, and felt proud: she had only to tread on them and they knew who she was. But her flesh crawled as well, just a little. Night-time wasn't the same as daytime, and who could be certain that the lavatory spirits didn't have relations on the staircase – cousins, perhaps, who gently sighed when you hurt them? She wished she had her shoes on. Although the nightshirt she'd put on in the parlour had been pleasantly warm from the stove, the chill was insidiously creeping upwards from the soles of her feet and taking up residence beneath the garment's folds like an uninvited guest. Her grandmother had undone her plaits in front of the stove, even though she'd long been able to do this by herself. Granny must think she was still a little child incapable of making stairs creak.

There was just enough light upstairs for her to find the door of her room and open it. She jumped, it creaked so loudly. More spirits were in evidence here – hinge-dwelling cousins of the spirits that haunted the staircase and lavatory. Quickly, she groped her way along the big bed and slipped between the sheets. Having expected them to be cold, she was relieved when her toes encountered a small bag of heated cherry stones; and, when she slightly raised the bedclothes between herself and her sleeping brother, the warmth that flowed to meet her suggested that a little tiled stove was burning there. She rubbed her legs together for a moment to drive away the cold completely, then pulled the sheet over her head until only her hair peeped out. At the thought of the unknown, invisible beings whose presence throughout the house had to be assumed, she burrowed down still further until even her hair disappeared under the covers. Before long, however, she ran short of air and cautiously poked her nose out. Finally she sat up, made a dent in the pillow, and settled her head in it.

Her caution seemed justified when, not long afterwards, the spirits of the staircase groaned and a glimmer of light danced up and down the cracks in the door. She dived back under the bedclothes and moved so close to Kaspar that their legs touched.

"Are you asleep, Didi?"

Katharina took the edge of the sheet in both hands and pulled it down to a point just below her eyes. Granny was standing in the doorway holding a candle that flickered restlessly in the draft.

"Nearly," Katharina murmured.

The old woman looked gigantic in the candlelight. Her nose was the size of a potato, or so it seemed to Katharina, and as she slowly approached the bed a huge, shadowy grandmother lurched across the ceiling.

"We haven't said our prayers yet," said Granny. There was nothing to put the candlestick on, so she folded her hands around it and recited in a low voice:

> God the Father, on your throne,
> And Jesus Christ, your only Son,

To you fervently we pray,
Bless this homestead day by day,
Bless all those who dwell therein
And your little child Kathrin.

"Amen," whispered Katharina. She had folded her hands on the bedclothes and was staring up at the ceiling. Above her was the attic, above that the roof itself, above that the rain clouds, above that the sky, and up in the sky the throne on which God the Father sat – which didn't, strangely enough, fall to earth although it must be very heavy, what with all the gold, silver and precious stones that adorned it. Perhaps it was permanently supported by angels who hovered in mid-air the way hawks did before swooping on their prey; and if Afra Bäbler had become an angel she would probably take her turn sometime. Wasn't it very cold up there? The higher you climbed the colder it got – in fact the Meer Glacier on the Hausstock never melted, even in the hottest of summers.

"Now let's think of your mother," Granny added, "and pray that she has a safe delivery."

Katharina's thoughts plummeted from the heavenly throne-room to the Meur. She was glad that the midwife with the red hair-ribbon had got there and was looking after Mama. How many babies would be born tonight all over the country? Or all over the world? How did God the Father and his son Jesus manage to help everyone who prayed to them? All right, so they didn't have to go to China, where the heathens lived, but there were plenty of Christians else-where, not only in the canton of Glarus but even in America.

Niklaus, Mama's brother, had emigrated to America. A letter from him had come last week and remained on the taproom counter for days, either beside or beneath the book with the list of unpaid bar bills, and Papa had shown the letter to everyone who wanted to see it and told them that Niklaus was now called Nick. Katharina hoped – and this horrid thought flashed through her head like a thunderbolt – that God the Father wouldn't be in America just when the baby was born. What if Jesus was also too busy to look in on Elm? If so, it was all to the good that Verena Elmer was there. Ought she to pray to Verena as well? Or for her, at least, so that God would give her strength even if he couldn't come himself? But perhaps he *would* come himself, or Jesus, or both of them. After all, Parson Mohr had said that God was everywhere. That was what was so special about him, and what she found so hard to imagine.

"Look at Kaspar, see how sound asleep he is," said Granny. "If he wakes up and needs to do a Thin Aunt, or if you do, there are two potties under the bed, one on each side."

Katharina nodded, remembering with distaste how she had already helped her little brother to do a Thin Aunt once today, and what the result had been. She dearly hoped he wouldn't wake before morning.

"Well, then," said Granny, and turned to go. Katharina had really been hoping that she would stroke her head the way Mama always did.

"Granny," she said, "did everything go all right when you had your babies?"

"Oh, yes," said Granny, "mine were no trouble."

"How many did you have?"

"Thirteen."

"That many?"

Katharina could scarcely believe it, though she now remembered having heard that figure sometime – thirteen, or rather, twelve. If Mama had as many babies as that, they would be getting as many brothers and sisters again as they already had, or even more. They were already sleeping four to a bed, so where would they all go? In the stable, like baby Jesus? It would be all right in summer, when the two cows and their calves were grazing on the high pastures, but difficulties would arise when they came down again. Maybe they would have to beg houseroom from the Rhyners next door.

"And none of them died?"

"Yes, one," said Granny. "Scarlet fever, when he was a year old. The other twelve are all grown up."

"What was he called, the one that died?"

Her grandmother sighed. "Kaspar."

"Kaspar?" Katharina was taken aback. "But I've got an uncle called Kaspar, haven't I?"

"He was born after the first one died. We tried again, that's all."

It was nice to be able to try again. Papa and Mama would probably try again if the new baby died. But how, exactly? There it was again, the question she dared not ask. It was at least as dangerous as asking how Grandfather died, and she wouldn't get an answer to it while her grandmother still undid her plaits, no matter how many thunderstorms she braved with little Kaspar's hand in hers.

"Well, then," the old woman repeated, and turned to go again.

"Granny," Katharina said quickly, "why does the track to the Bleiggen go through the middle of a house?"

Granny laughed. "The questions you ask!" she said. "The track always ran that way until someone built a house over it, and when the district council realised that the house was sitting plumb on top of a right-of-way, they ordered the owner to let anyone going from the Bleiggen to the village or from the village to the Bleiggen walk straight through it. That still applies to this day."

Katharina remembered the muffled coughing behind the door and the voice that had spoken of the Flood. She was glad no right-of-way ran through the Meur and let anyone who wanted climb *their* stairs. Having all those strangers in the taproom was bad enough.

Kaspar gave a long sigh and sat up beside her. Blinking in the candlelight, he looked at his grandmother and his sister in turn. His lips trembled, his eyes filled with tears.

"Go back to sleep," Katharina told him, plumping up his pillow. "We're at Granny's."

The little boy continued to sit there as if debating whether it would be worth his while to cry. Katharina stroked his head and said: "You mustn't be frightened." That clinched his decision – he wouldn't cry after all. Instead, he would rest his head on the nice soft pillow, look at his sister, let his eyelids droop, and instantly fall asleep again.

"There's a good child," said her grandmother. "Good-night."

"Granny," said Katharina, "how did the . . . "

"Ssh, Didi." Granny put a finger to her lips. "Goodnight now."

"Goodnight," Katharina whispered.

She watched the little flame glide to the door followed by the shadowy giantess, who was suddenly swallowed up by the darkness. The door closed, and this time it seemed to Katharina that the spirits were squeaking with delight because they now had two children in their clutches. She wished her grandmother had left the door open a crack; then she might have been able to see a faint glow of light from the kitchen.

But she didn't dare get out of bed and open it. She was a good child, her grandmother had just said so. Or had she meant Kaspar?

Katharina strained her ears. Laughter could be heard coming from the kitchen, but it sounded very distant, as if its source were in another country altogether. The spirits of the staircase complained under Granny's weight, the kitchen door closed, the laughter died.

The silence was absolute now. All Katharina could hear was her brother's breathing and her own heartbeat.

"*I'm* the good child," she told herself, "so I mustn't be frightened."

After a while her heart pounded less furiously and it started to rain outside. A gust of wind drove the raindrops against the window panes. Katharina thought of the Flood. She had wanted to ask her grandmother how the story ended. It was in the Bible, after all, and had nothing to do with goitres or making babies. Not everyone could have drowned, surely, or there wouldn't be anyone alive today.

There was a distant crash. She hoped it wasn't a rockfall, but what else could it be?

She thought of the Meur and how everyone would now be waiting for the baby to be born, Papa down in the taproom with Anna and Jakob and Regula, Mama panting and sweating upstairs in her bedroom with the midwife, Züsi in her little lair beneath the stairs. Hurriedly clasping her hands together, she offered up a silent prayer: "Dear God, keep that rock from falling on top of the Meur."

Before she could unclasp her hands there was another crash. "Dear Lord Jesus," she went on quickly, "throw that one into the river!"

Jesus was the son of God, so he was bound to enjoy damming streams or throwing stones into them like her brother Jakob and his friends, and being all-powerful he could also hurl a whole rock into the river if he had a mind to, and the spray would shoot high into the air – so high that it would come down over the valley like rain, like the rain that was drumming incessantly on the window panes.

8

SOMEWHERE IN THE HOUSE, A WOMAN'S VOICE COULD be heard singing an old nursery rhyme:

> Good morrow, good morrow!
> Chirped little cock sparrow.

The first thing Katharina noticed on waking was that she had left her doll downstairs. She always took Lisi to bed as a rule, but last night everything had been different. She hadn't returned to the parlour after going to the lavatory, so the poor little thing was probably still sitting on the sofa, waiting for her.

Daylight was filtering through the crack between the shutters. Katharina felt relieved that the night was over and revelled in having so much bed to herself. Kaspar was still asleep beside her. She stretched, and the tips of her toes collided with the bag of cherry stones, now cold. As she withdrew her foot slightly, she noticed that the undersheet was damp. Lifting the bedclothes an inch or two, she peered beneath them and saw a big damp patch that gave off a smell of warm wee-wee. So her little brother had done it in the bed after all.

She wondered whether there was anything she could do

about it. No, there was nothing to be done, absolutely nothing. She remembered Kaspar waking up briefly while she was chatting with her grandmother. Granny could have sat him on the pot then. And she herself had slept solidly until now.

The thought of the chamber pot provoked a sudden, over-powering twinge in the pit of her stomach. Not wanting to go downstairs until someone came to fetch her, she got out of bed, pulled out the pot, and sat on it. The jet hit the bottom of the vessel with a high-pitched tinkle that gave way to a sound like the splashing of a fountain, then she was done. Quickly pushing the pot back under the bed, Katharina went to the window.

She unlatched the windows, hooked them back, and pushed both shutters open. For a moment she involuntarily shut her eyes tight.

The landscape might have been freshly washed. Everything was wet and glistening: the meadows, the trees, the rock faces on the other side of the valley, the forests and crests. Numerous little clouds clung to the slopes like mislaid handkerchiefs. Only patches of blue sky could be seen. Most of the peaks were hidden by clouds in constant motion.

On the ridge opposite she made out the Martinsloch, the rocky arch through which the sun shone down on Elm twice a year as it rose. The last time, in spring, she and the other second-formers had stationed themselves on the slope behind the church and watched the sun's rays strike first the steeple, then the roofs of the village and all who were standing there. Then the sun was blotted out, to reappear a little later when it cleared the crest.

Katharina had enjoyed that, and the teacher had said how rare a phenomenon it was. There was nothing like it anywhere else in Switzerland – in fact people had come specially from Zurich and St Gallen and put up at the Gasthaus Elmer overnight, just to catch this brief glimpse of the sun through the Martinsloch. The same thing happened the following day, but one had to wait another six months before it happened again. It couldn't be long now, thought Katharina, and she hoped it wouldn't be raining when the time came.

The teacher had also explained why the sun didn't always rise in the same place. It had to do with the fact that the days became longer and shorter and that the stars and the earth itself were always in motion, though you'd never know it when you opened the shutters in the morning.

The sun must have risen by now, but it was lurking somewhere high above the clouds.

Katharina looked across at the sheer face of the Plattenberg. Some little grey clouds were sprouting from it, almost like the puffs of smoke that appeared when the quarrymen were blasting. Could she see where all the noise had come from yesterday? All that caught her eye was a line of fir trees high up in the Tschingelwald. They were leaning over at such an angle, they seemed to have been transfixed in the act of falling down. Perhaps they were the ones that stood beside the Great Chlagg, the crevice of which two herdsmen had spoken in the taproom. It was so deep, they said, you could toss a pebble into it and never hear it hit the bottom.

"You don't believe that yourself!" a purple-nosed farmer had bellowed from behind his glass of schnapps. When one of the herdsmen suggested he went up there for a look, the farmer said he had more sense. Then Peter Elmer loudly declared that if the farmer did go up there he'd probably be so drunk he'd fall down the Chlagg himself, and no one could fail to hear *him* hit the bottom. At that, the purple-nosed farmer sprang to his feet, knocking over the table he was sitting at and smashing his glass on the floor, and everyone else stood up too, glaring at each other, and if Papa hadn't stepped between them in the nick of time and growled at them to go outside if they wanted to fight, there would definitely have been a free-for-all.

Katharina, who was no stranger to such brawls, used to get up at once and make for the door to the stairs so as to be able to beat a retreat if necessary. With a mixture of fear and curiosity she'd watch the men grappling. She wouldn't scamper upstairs until bottles started flying through the air.

There were also occasions when young men came to blows outside the inn after Papa had locked up for the night. The last time it happened Jakob and Regula had woken Katharina and the three of them had watched from their window, giggling, as two men exchanged blows, egged on by a small circle of spectators who moved across the fore-court, this way and that, as the fighting progressed. By the time Papa came out to chase the youths away, which he eventually did, one of them was bleeding from the mouth. Each group surrounded its champion and set off in the direction of the iron bridge. Their receding figures steadily dwindled but their mutual insults seemed to bounce off the moon and reverberate for a long time afterwards.

The Meur and Untertal were invisible from Granny's house, being hidden by the strip of forest below it. Not a soul could be seen on the track that led to the village. Katharina looked down at the little garden beneath her window, in which red and yellow flowers were growing beside the lettuce beds and two hens clucked softly as they went in search of seeds. In one corner, some huge rhubarb leaves almost overtopped the garden fence.

Katharina shivered in the chill morning air. Looking across once more at the peaks and crests, she wondered if the sun would come out today. A little cloud issued from the Martinsloch like vapour billowing from a dragon's nostril. Then the rocky arch completely vanished and clouds and mist billowed down from above until not even a speck of blue sky remained. A plume of smoke drifted down the track from the house. There was a smell of burning wood.

Katharina shut the window and slipped back into bed. She snuggled right up to the edge to avoid coming into contact with the damp patch, but the nasty smell seeped through the bedclothes and wouldn't go away.

She listened intently. Who was up already?

Something clattered in the kitchen – a fire iron, perhaps, or the door of the stove or a saucepan lid.

Then the kitchen door opened and she heard Granny say: "See you later, Paul." Soon afterwards the front door creaked

68

open and Nero started barking, but he was quickly silenced by her uncle's reassuring voice. Not a sound came from baby Anna, now that Margret had sung her a morning lullaby. Where was Margret, anyway?

The floorboards creaked outside the door. Suddenly recalling her fears of last night, Katharina couldn't understand why she had been so scared. Weren't the noises the same? No, they weren't: a noise shrouded in darkness was quite different from a noise heard in daylight. The door hinges seemed to emit a cheerful groan as Margret looked in and said: "Well, what are our two sleepyheads up to?"

"I'm awake," Katharina said quickly.

She was a little disappointed that it wasn't Granny who had come to wake them. Margret was already dressed in a blue frock with a brown and white striped apron over it. She had pinned up her hair, but not the way Granny did. To Katharina it looked more like a bird's nest.

"What about him?" asked Margret, nodding in the direction of Kaspar.

"He's done it in the bed," said Katharina.

Margret laughed. "Oh dear, then we'll have to change the sheet. I've got to wash some nappies today in any case. It can go in with them."

Kaspar wriggled out of bed and stood up, looking bemusedly from Margret to his sister. "Want to wee-wee," he said.

"Here." Margret stooped and dragged his pot from under the bed.

Kaspar pulled down his underpants, sat on it, and weed. Then he farted and a Fat Aunt splashed into the pot. Instantly the whole room reeked of it. Katharina pulled a face.

"I'm wet," said Kaspar, getting to his feet.

"Yes," said Katharina, "you did it in the bed."

He shook his head, but she folded back the bedclothes far enough to reveal the damp patch. "That's what potties are for," she said sternly.

Kaspar stared at the stained sheet in bewilderment, unable to perceive any connection between the damp patch and himself.

"Come on, Kaspar," said Margret, taking him by the hand, "let's go downstairs and get you dressed. And you," she said, turning to Katharina, "empty those potties, then put some clothes on."

When Margret and Kaspar had gone downstairs, Katharina briefly debated whether to empty the chamber pots out of the window without more ado, but she didn't dare. She resented being landed with such a distasteful job. She had to do it at home, though, so why should she be any better off here?

Pursing her lips she picked up first her own pot, then her brother's, and carried them gingerly downstairs to the lavatory, where she put them on the floor, removed the lid and emptied them in turn down the stinking hole. They had to be rinsed out as well, and that, she knew, would also be expected of her.

She stuffed the laces loosely into her shoes and slipped them on. A growl came from the kennel when she opened the front door.

"Good dog, Nero," she said, nervously tiptoeing past the dog, which rested its head on its paws but never took its eyes off her. She held the chamber pots under the fountain, then sluiced her hands and face as well. The cold pervaded her fingers and cheeks and transmitted itself to the rest of her body. Quickly retrieving the chamber pots, she ran back into the house, left them and her shoes at the foot of the stairs, and made her way through the kitchen to the parlour, where she promptly knelt down on the sofa and nestled against the warm slate stove. Her wooden doll was still sitting there.

"Poor Lisi," she said. "All by yourself on the sofa all night. Weren't you frightened?"

"No," she squeaked in a dolly's voice, "I'm not a scaredy-cat."

"I know," said Katharina, "you're a very brave girl. Would you like to sleep outside with Nero tonight?"

"No, with you," squeaked Lisi.

Kaspar, who was just having yesterday's shirt pulled over his head by Margret, had been listening to this conversation with glee. "And with me," he said, hopping up and down.

"Only if you don't wet the bed," said Lisi. "Do you hear?" Kaspar's face fell.

"Won't wet the bed," he grumbled.

"Promise?" Lisi insisted.

He nodded.

"You'd better not," said Lisi, "or I'll bite off your willy."

"No!" he exclaimed in horror.

"Yes, I will," Lisi whispered implacably.

"No, you mustn't!" wailed Kaspar.

"That's enough, children," said Margret. Turning to

Katharina, she told her to put on her clothes, which were hanging beside the stove, and then come to the kitchen. "And what about those plaits of yours?"

"Where's Granny?" Katharina asked.

"Granny went back to bed, she's feeling rather poorly. Never mind, I'll help you with them after breakfast."

Katharina pulled on her knickers, then stripped off her nightshirt and donned her vest. The clothes felt wonderfully warm after a night beside the stove. She wondered if her grandmother was ill, but what she most wanted to know was whether she'd plaited her hair and pinned it up, or whether she was lying in bed with her hair loose and whether it made her look different, the way Mama had looked yesterday. Suddenly reminded of the reason for her presence at Granny's, she went into the kitchen in her underclothes and asked Margret if the baby had arrived.

"We haven't heard yet," said Margret. She told Katharina not to wander around looking like a plucked chicken but to finish getting dressed and then come and sit down beside Kaspar, who was already seated in front of a slice of bread and a bowl of hot milk tinged with a dash of coffee.

9

"NO, THOSE AREN'T OUR HENS," SAID MARGRET. SHE
and Katharina were leaning out of the parlour window,
looking down at the garden. "All ours are speckled." She
clapped her hands and hissed, "Be off with you!", and
Katharina clapped and hissed too.

The two white hens retreated, clucking, to the rhubarb
leaves beside the fence. They put their heads on one side
and looked reproachfully up at the house.

Kaspar jostled Katharina from behind. "Want to see!"

Katharina pushed him away but Margret bent down,
hoisted him by his armpits and set him down in front of
her on the window sill, which he clung to with both hands.

"Psst, psst!" he hissed. Then he asked: "Where are they?"

"Over there by the rhubarb," said Katharina, and added
quietly but distinctly: "Blind bat!"

"Not a blind bat," Kaspar retorted. "Psst, psst!" he hissed
again, this time in the right direction. "Go away!"

But the hens remained where they were, indignantly
clucking to themselves.

"They must have escaped from Barbara's," Margret said
to Katharina. "All her hens are white. You'd better run and
tell her."

Katharina was dressed by now. She had put on the lavender blue dress borrowed from Granny's cupboard with her own brown pinafore over it. Margret had told her she could wear the Sunday best she'd arrived in tomorrow – it wasn't Sunday till then in any case. Her plaits, which had been braided but not pinned up, were dangling over her shoulders. All she had to do was put her shoes on, then she could go.

She sat down on the little bench in the hall. Her first attempt to tie a bow was a failure. She looked round in search of help, but then it occurred to her that anyone capable of making stairs creak could also tie her own shoelaces, and she promptly managed two nice bows. It wasn't until both shoes were on that she noticed the chamber pots standing at the foot of the stairs. She decided to take them upstairs when she got back.

Barbara's house was just up the track from Granny's. Katharina wasn't keen to go, for all that. She'd been looking forward to a little holiday, if the truth be told, but no sooner had she got here than she was made to do things. Kaspar didn't have to come with her, of course – he was allowed to stay in the warm parlour with Margret. At home she was sometimes sent to fetch eggs from Elsbeth when they'd run out and needed some in the taproom, but that wasn't the same. She knew Elsbeth, who always smelt of her husband's tobacco. Her husband was Old Jaggli, who coughed the whole time because he always had a pipe in his mouth. He was known as Old Jaggli to distinguish him from Young Jaggli, who lived in Untertal on the way to the iron bridge and the Meur. Katharina also knew Young Jaggli and his wife, though she'd never had to fetch eggs from them, and she even knew "young" Elsbeth, their grown-up daughter, who had no husband and consequently no children, which may have had something to do with the goitre that clung to her neck like a toad. Katharina wondered if she would some day die of it the way Grandfather had. The likeliest way to die of a goitre was for it to swell up, bigger and bigger, until you couldn't breathe. Katharina clutched her throat in horror at the thought of it.

She had reached a little bend in the track and could already see the roof of the house the hens belonged to.

Katharina disliked visiting strangers, and she scarcely knew Barbara. All she knew was that she was the mother of Hans-Kaspar, who had gone behind the Meur with Anna and come into the kitchen last night. Barbara was also the mother of Lena, a schoolmate of Katharina's. Lena's father was dead, and she always went around barefoot. Katharina had once seen her coming out of the poorhouse carrying a bowl of soup.

If Lena didn't have a father, she reasoned, then Barbara didn't have a husband, so who looked after the farm?

A cow was standing beside the track, staring at her.

Katharina thought of her family's cows, Bless and Stern, which were up on the Falzüber Alp with their calves. The Meur got its milk from the third cow, Lobe, the only one to remain at home in summer. Bless and Stern would be back in another two weeks, Papa had said not long ago, and she wondered how much their calves would have grown.

Only one cow had remained behind at Granny's farm too, for the milk. Her name was Blüemli and Katharina had watched Uncle Paul milking her last night. The others were up on the Alp, but she didn't know how many of them there were.

When she turned down the path that led to the house, which lay in a dip, a dog outside started barking. She stopped short.

A woman emerged from the barn beside the house and looked round. The bleached skull of a cow, one horn pointing downwards, hung crookedly from a nail above the barn door. The woman had now caught sight of her.

"What do you want?" she called.

She obviously didn't know who Katharina was. Two little boys came out of the front door and stared up the path. The dog had run over to the woman and continued to bark incessantly at her side.

It was a moment before Katharina remembered why she had come. "I'm Katharina," she called back.

The woman was still at a loss. "What?"

She probably takes me for a beggar child, thought Katharina, that's why she isn't holding her noisy dog by the collar. It was hard to make herself heard above the din.

"I've come from Granny," she shouted as loudly as she could, trying to remember what Granny's first name was, because Granny was Granny to her but not to the woman down there, who must be Barbara. But Barbara had evidently grasped who Katharina was. She took her dog by the collar, walked him to the kennel, and chained him up. "You can come now," she called.

Katharina walked down the path to the house, where the woman stood waiting for her in an incredibly dirty apron, one little boy clinging to her skirt on either side. The woman's dress was full of holes, and the sandals on her bare feet were tied together with string. With a far from friendly expression she asked if Katharina was Didi from the Meur, where a baby was expected.

Katharina nodded, then told her as quickly as possible that there were two white hens in Granny's garden and Margret thought they must come from here.

"Why from here?" Barbara demanded brusquely, and Katharina told her that Granny only had speckled hens. "I'd be surprised if two of mine have got away," Barbara said. "I haven't opened the henhouse. Joseph!" she called through the doorway, but when no one appeared she muttered something like "lazy brute", told Katharina to follow her and shuffled round the house followed by the two boys, whose legs were caked with grime to the knee.

When Katharina saw the decrepit henhouse, which was not much taller than herself, she immediately spotted two badly patched holes in the chicken wire. Any hen could have got out, no matter how carefully the door was bolted.

"Can you count?" Barbara asked abruptly.

Katharina nodded and counted the hens, which had clustered together at her approach, clucking in alarm. "Six," she said.

Barbara had counted them too. "So they're all here. You can tell Anna those birds aren't mine."

Anna . . . of course! That was Granny's name, Katharina remembered now.

Barbara shuffled back to the house with the boys toddling silently along beside her. Katharina followed them, stepping over the hay rakes and pitchforks strewn around on the ground. As she walked behind Barbara she thought she caught the strange herbal smell of schnapps, which puzzled her because women didn't drink schnapps. The smaller of the boys was wearing a shirt that came down to just above his knees. Nearly all the way down the back was a rent through which Katharina glimpsed bare flesh. He hasn't got a vest on, she thought.

"Not at school?" Barbara asked, looking over her shoulder.

Katharina was perplexed. "No," she said quietly. Any fool could see she was here and not at school.

They had reached the kennel again. The dog gave a suspicious growl.

"Quiet, damn you!" Barbara shouted, so fiercely that Katharina jumped. The animal promptly cowered down and slunk into its kennel. Part of the roof was missing. Barbara paused. "Has the baby come?"

Katharina thought for a moment before answering. "We don't know yet." Then she added: "Verena went to her yesterday."

Barbara sighed. "Another mouth to feed."

One of the little boys opened his mouth for the first time and asked for something to eat. "You're not getting anything now, wait till midday," Barbara snapped. He started to whimper but she stood there unmoved and said no more.

"I'll say goodbye, then," said Katharina, and quickly set off up the path.

Just as she turned out on to the track Barbara called after her in a strident voice: "Tell Anna, if those hens don't belong to anyone, I'll have them."

Katharina raised one hand to show she'd understood. It struck her only now that no smoke was rising from Barbara's chimney. A gaunt youngster slunk out from behind the barn and watched her depart, only to receive an earful of abuse from Barbara. That must be Joseph the lazy brute, Katharina told herself, walking faster, anxious to get away as soon as possible. If Margret sent her there again she wouldn't go.

Feeling rather cold, she stuck her hands in the pockets of her pinafore and came across her mother's dried plums. She had a vision of the hungry little boy. Why hadn't she given him one?

She'd only just noticed that she had the plums, that was one reason, and Barbara would have been angry, that was another; and besides, the other boy would have wanted one too. That made three answers to one question, and three were more than enough. She walked on quickly, making for her grandmother's house, which was now in sight. It was starting to spit with rain. No sun again after all.

It was bad when your husband died, she reflected. You had holes everywhere – in your clothes, in the henhouse, in the kennel – and hay rakes lay strewn around and your children had no shoes or stockings and had to go to the poorhouse for soup. It was best not to have a husband at all, like Elsbeth the daughter of Young Jaggli, then no one could die on you and some other member of the family would care for the children. Whole families inhabited the homes of Young Jaggli and Old Jaggli, and one of Young Jaggli's sons, also called Jaggli, went to school with her – he was in the first form – and one of Old Jaggli's sons, another Jaggli, was in the third form, and they both had older and younger brothers and sisters; and sometimes they all played blind man's buff together outside the Meur or hide-and-seek beside the Raminer and they had much more fun than Barbara's children did up here.

Nero barked when he heard Katharina coming. She wondered why he was so loath to recognize her.

"Good dog, Nero," she said soothingly when she got near him, but he continued to bark. Then, remembering Barbara, she shouted, "Quiet, damn you!", and to her astonishment he promptly stopped barking and lay down inside his kennel.

"You forgot the chamber pots," Margret told her a few moments later, as she was pulling off her shoes in the hall.

"I was just going to take them upstairs."

"You don't say," Margret retorted rather sharply.

"No, honestly," said Katharina, "I had my shoes on before." Why didn't grown-ups ever believe you? When she grew up she would always believe children when they said they meant to take the potties upstairs.

"Well, what about those hens?"

"They don't belong to Barbara. Hers are all there, I counted them myself."

"How many were there?"

"Six," Katharina said proudly.

She could be relied on when it wasn't a question of something as silly as chamber pots. She could be sent to call on strangers by herself, and she could even count their hens.

Margret shook her head. "That's odd," she said.

10

"AND THEN, WHEN THE DOVE FAILED TO RETURN AND he saw that there was dry land beneath him, Noah and all his family left the Ark and landed on Mount Ararat, and God made a big rainbow appear in the sky to show that he wanted to be at peace with mankind once more."

"What about the animals?"

"They all came walking out of the Ark and spread across the face of the earth."

Katharina, seated at the parlour table with her back to the window, was listening to her grandmother, who was stretched out on the sofa beside the stove.

Granny had got up again towards midday and made some soup with turnips and pearl barley in it. Earlier, Margret had washed the nappies and the sheet in the fountain and hung them up to dry in the barn with Katharina's help. The spots of rain she'd felt on the way back from Barbara's had developed into a regular downpour.

Paul, compelled to stop work on his second crop of hay when the rain came down, had returned home in a bad mood. The inhabitants of Elm were obviously in the Almighty's bad books, he'd said at lunch, perhaps because they'd got rid of the old hymnal. Granny reproved him, but Paul said he was sure the Almighty could take a joke, and what did Didi think? That earned him a rebuke from his wife. He shouldn't ask a child such questions, Margret told him, and Katharina was glad of that because she didn't know the answer.

After lunch Granny sucked a lump of sugar with a few drops of valerian on it, and the children were also allowed to help themselves to a sugar lump from the tin with flowers and curlicues on it. Then Kaspar was sent off to bed for his afternoon rest. He wanted to take Lisi with him, but Katharina put her foot down and sat the wooden doll on the bench behind the stove in the parlour. Granny lay down on the sofa for a rest. She didn't know what was the matter with her, she said. She simply didn't feel well, but it would pass. Then Katharina asked how the Flood had ended, and Granny told her the whole story over again.

Katharina loved listening to her grandmother telling stories. Her parents seldom found the time. Whenever she asked them a question they tended to answer it as briefly as possible because they always happened to have something else to do.

The story of how General Suvorov and his Russian army had crossed the Panixer Pass she knew mainly from her grandmother, who once told her how thousands of ragged, starving soldiers had marched up the valley and into the village, and how they took all five cows from Old Rhyner's cowshed and slaughtered them in the yard and fell on the raw meat at once because they couldn't bring themselves to wait until they'd roasted it, and how the beasts' entrails had steamed in the cold air, and how the soldiers' faces were red with blood after their grisly meal, and how others had even tossed dried goatskins into boiling water in the hope of making soup out of them, and how they tore the clothes from the villagers' bodies and the shoes from their feet, and how the Russians were under constant fire from their French pursuers, and how General Suvorov had spent the night at the Landvogt's house, and how Granny's father, who was then a young lad, had been made to take a lantern and go with the Russians at dawn the next day and guide them to the Panixer Pass, and how it had snowed without a break, and how the whole of the upper valley was so filled with windblown clouds and mist you could scarcely see the man in front of you, and how the snow in the Jetzloch was so deep that even Johann Bäbler, Blind Meinrad's father, who spent each summer as a dairyman on the Oberstafel, had difficulty in finding the path, and how it became steadily colder as they neared the pass, and how scores of soldiers, many of whom had nothing but strips of cloth on their feet, slipped and fell screaming over the precipices together with their mules and the cannon they were hauling, and how the horses whinnied in despair as they slipped and fell to their death, and how the heavy cannon thundered down the slopes, turning over and over, and how whole columns of men were buried beneath snowslides and avalanches, and how many of them simply collapsed, too exhausted to get up again, and how darkness descended on the pass and the cavalrymen with their curved sabres and long, dark beards burnt their lances to keep the general warm in his grey greatcoat and black tricorne hat,

84

and how Granny's father and old Bäbler had snuffed out their lanterns and sneaked back down to the valley under cover of darkness, threading their way through the freezing soldiers, and how Blind Meinrad still wore the thick fur cap his father had worn on the Panixer . . . and who could tell? said Granny: if her own father hadn't turned back he might also have lost his life somewhere up there in the snow, and she herself would never have been born, so her Schaaggli wouldn't have been born either, and neither would Katharina.

Katharina had shivered at the thought, and she shivered again at the recollection of it. So if Granny's father hadn't turned back, she wouldn't be here at all . . .

"Granny," she said abruptly, "your father wasn't a coward, was he?"

Her grandmother looked disconcerted. "Whatever put that into your head?"

"I mean, because he turned back instead of crossing the pass with General Suvorov?"

No, said Granny, her father had been a brave man. Why should he have risked his life for the Russians' sake? They'd looted the entire village, after all, and turning back was dangerous in any case, because anyone caught running away would have been shot out of hand.

"And Noah?" Katharina asked. "Wasn't Noah a coward either?"

Her grandmother was more astonished still. "What do you mean?"

"Everyone laughed at him for building his Ark on dry land."

85

"Yes," said Granny, who had just told her that, "but Noah knew he had to build the Ark because he'd been warned to do so by God himself."

So they weren't cowards at all, neither Granny's father nor Noah. Each had in some way known better than everyone else: the former knew it was becoming more and more dangerous up there in the mountains, and the latter had been told by God that disaster lay in store for mankind. It was preferable, of course, to have it straight from God on his heavenly throne.

"Granny," said Katharina, "how did God tell Noah to build the Ark? Did he come down to earth himself?"

Her grandmother sighed. "I think Noah must have prayed so hard that God appeared to him in a vision," she said. "That way, he could tell him in person."

Now it was Katharina's turn to sigh. Perhaps she should have prayed so hard yesterday that God appeared to *her* in a vision. Then he could have told her right away that all would be well with Mama and the new baby, or that he would send his son to look in on them.

"Granny," she said, but the sound of deep, regular breathing from the sofa told her that her grandmother had dozed off. She'd meant to ask her whether the baby had been born yet, but how could her grandmother know since no one had come to tell her? Should she herself walk down to Untertal and see if it had happened? As soon as Granny woke up she would ask her. Katharina turned and looked out of the window. She could just see the Plattenberg, which was overhung by a dense mass of cloud. A gust of wind fired a volley of raindrops at the window pane. She heard the baby whimpering upstairs, then Margret's soothing voice, then silence. Paul was out. He had returned to the upper pasture to patch the haystack. Fridolin had accompanied Johannes to the joiner's shop in the village. Both had promised to look in at the Meur after work and bring back the latest news. There wasn't a sound from Kaspar, who seemed to be asleep.

Katharina tiptoed over to the doll's house that stood on the floor beside the door to Granny's bedroom. It was the doll's house her father and all his brothers and sisters had played with as children, and Granny had got it out especially for her and Kaspar.

If you folded back the roof you could see into the rooms: a parlour, two bedrooms, a kitchen, and behind the kitchen a storeroom with shelves on which lay some tiny sacks. Hanging against the wall of the storeroom there were little wax models of hams and bundles of painted matchsticks representing sausages. The inhabitants of the doll's house were little white animals' bones dressed up in tiny clothes to make them look like people. The smallest bone lay in a cradle beside the bed in one of the bedrooms. The cradle was carved out of wood, and you could even rock it. Katharina prodded it gently with her forefinger and sang in a low voice:

> Sleep, baby, sleep,
> The stars are shining bright.

But the little bone was fretful. It snuffled beneath its woollen blanket. There was only one thing to do: fetch its mother, who was seated at the kitchen table with a miniature

87

saucepan beside her, making bean soup out of pine needles. Katharina carried her over to the baby and opened her blue blouse, which was fastened with a single button. Then she pressed the baby's head against the place where its mother's breast had to be, and a soft sucking sound made itself heard.

Katharina thought of the women's breasts she'd seen yesterday. She found it hard to imagine that something of the kind would one day grow on her and fill up with mother's milk. But this was inevitable, it seemed, for her sister Regula's bosom was definitely starting to swell and Anna's breasts were at least as big as their mother's, so her own turn would come in due course.

There was a crash outside. Katharina dropped the mother and child and ran to the window. She scanned the whole of the Plattenberg, but there was no sign that anything had just broken off. That was the trouble with rockfalls: the rocks had already landed by the time you heard the crash; you never saw one actually breaking off.

For all that, she thought she detected a little grey plume of smoke at the spot where the fir trees were leaning over sideways. Had some of them fallen down the Great Chlagg, the crevice that was so deep the herdsmen couldn't hear stones land when they dropped them down it?

"What was that, Didi?" Granny asked from the sofa.

"The mountain just swallowed some trees," she replied.

In the bedroom upstairs, Kaspar started to cry.

II

KATHARINA AND HER BROTHER WERE STANDING behind the cowshed. It stood at the back of Granny's house, and visible in the meadows further up the mountainside were barns, hedges, and clumps of trees. The rain had stopped, and Kaspar had said he wanted to see the pigs. Behind the cowshed was a small pigpen with a fenced enclosure that extended a little way up the slope. The surface of the enclosure was badly churned up, especially at the lower end, where a number of piglets were squealing as they wallowed in the stinking morass. The big sow was right at the top of the pen, but when she saw the children walk up to the fence she lumbered downhill towards them at a surprising rate, only pulling up at the very last moment. Katharina shrieked and leapt aside, whereas Kaspar hopped up and down with delight.

"You great big mummy pig!" he chortled. When the animal thrust its moist, inquisitive snout between the uprights, he squatted down, uprooted a dock plant and held it to the sow's nostrils. She backed away with a grunt and trotted off to join her young, which promptly hemmed her in on all sides.

Katharina felt annoyed. Why had she been so scared when

Kaspar hadn't? The way the sow had come charging towards them, she might have squashed them both. There was no telling if the fence would have held.

Kaspar climbed on to the lowest rail. "Come here, mummy pig," he crowed, waving the dock plant; but the sow declined his invitation, so he threw it at her.

The sow had lain down on her side in the mud and the piglets were fighting over her teats, squealing shrilly. When they were all sucking away in a contented row, Kaspar said: "Want something to eat." Getting down off the fence, he walked back round the cowshed to the forecourt with the fountain in the middle.

"Granny," he called loudly.

Katharina, who had followed him, told him to shut up. Their grandmother might be asleep, she wasn't feeling too well today.

Kaspar stood his ground. "Margret," he called just as loudly and made for the front door with resolute tread. Katharina snapped at him to stop shouting, then accompanied him into the hall, where she removed their shoes.

Granny was already standing in the kitchen doorway. She asked if they'd seen the piglets.

"Yes, all five of them," Katharina said quickly.

"They were drinking," Kaspar chimed in. "I'm hungry," he added.

"I see," Granny said with a smile. "Then we'll have to see what we can do." She led the children into the kitchen. There was some soup left over from lunch, she said. Should she heat it up again? Kaspar looked crestfallen. He was hungry because he'd hardly touched his soup at lunch, and he'd hardly touched it because he didn't *like* soup.

"Well, then," said Granny, "what else can I find for our little Sweet-Tooth?" Going over to the herb and spice shelf, she took a handful of dried pear slices from a little bag and put them on the table. Kaspar promptly grabbed some with both hands, but Granny, seeing Katharina's horrified expression, said they were meant for his sister as well. Katharina, too, grabbed some two-handed.

"No squabbling, children," said Granny, "there's enough for both of you." She nodded when Katharina asked if she might count the slices, so Katharina dealt them out like cards, starting with herself. There were eleven in all. Kaspar, spotting at once that the eleventh slice had ended up on her side, reached for it, but she fended him off with her hand. "How do you divide eleven by two?" she asked.

"Like this," said Granny. She picked up the disputed slice and popped it into her mouth.

While the children were chewing away she resumed her place at the table and went on peeling potatoes with a kitchen knife. She left the peelings on the table and placed the potatoes in a bowl.

"These are for supper," she said. "We always have potato mash on Saturdays."

Katharina wasn't overjoyed. She had really been hoping for boiled ham or some other kind of meat, the way there usually was when she visited her grandmother on New Year's Day, but she nodded when Granny asked if she liked it. At least she preferred mash with potato to mash with herb cheese. It was the smell of the herb cheese she found most repulsive of all.

Granny belched.

"I can't think what's the matter with me," she said. "I feel so queasy all the time."

"Wonderdrops," said Katharina.

"What?"

"Wonderdrops," Katharina repeated. "You ought to take some."

Granny said she only had tincture of valerian and she'd already taken some of that. What were these Wonder-drops?

The pedlar from Appenzell brought them, said Katharina, the one who sold people pills and potions in the parlour at the Meur. It was always a red-letter day when the little man with the big pack on his back turned up. The inn was filled with people waiting to be admitted to the parlour one by one, and Katharina particularly liked those days because the men in the taproom were often outnumbered by women.

Nonsense, said Granny, she didn't need any quack's remedies; valerian had been good enough for her mother and her grandmother before her. As if to underline this, she took a little flask from the kitchen cupboard and opened the sugar canister. Kaspar materialised beside her. "Want one too," he said. Granny popped a little piece of sugar into his mouth, put one on a spoon, trickled some valerian on it, and waited for the sugar to disintegrate into brown crumbs.

"What about me?" said Katharina.

"You're a big girl," Granny told her. "You should know better than to ask."

She put the spoon in her mouth and swallowed the contents with an expressionless face.

Katharina was outraged. Just because she could go to Barbara's on her own and knew how to count hens and pigs and slices of pear, she wasn't allowed a sugar lump; whereas Kaspar, who could only wet the bed and make a sow go away by tickling her nose with dock leaves, got treated to one.

"All right," said Granny, who had noticed her resentment, "take one." And she held out the tin.

Blushing, Katharina helped herself to a piece and mumbled a thank-you. It irked her that her grandmother had read her thoughts, and the piece of sugar dissolving on her tongue seemed to taste less sweet than the one after lunch.

"Want another," pleaded Kaspar, but Granny was already replacing the tin in the kitchen cupboard.

"Eat your pear, lad," she said, and did another belch. Her stomach was rumbling audibly. She pressed her hand against her apron, shaking her head, and sat down again.

Margret came into the kitchen with baby Anna in her arms.

"How are you, Mother?" she asked.

"I'm noisy today."

"I'll make you some herb tea, it'll do you good. I'll join you, and I'm sure the children will have some too, won't you, Didi?"

Katharina nodded, but Kaspar got up and went over to the door to the parlour. "Want to play," he said, "with the dolly's house."

Katharina watched him go suspiciously. Was it safe to

leave him alone with the doll's house? He was quite capable of breaking a doll or dropping one and treading on it. She glanced enquiringly at her grandmother, but Granny obviously had no objection and didn't tell her to go and supervise him, so she remained sitting with the two grown-ups.

"Would you hold Anna for me?" Margret asked, and handed her the baby without waiting for an answer. Katharina cautiously took the little thing, which tried to kick itself free and followed Margret with its eyes as she bent down, opened the door of the stove, and put in two pieces of firewood. Margret told Anna not to be frightened: Mama was here, after all, and Didi was taking take care of her. She ladled some water into a saucepan from the tub, fetched a tin of dried herbs from the shelf and sprinkled a handful on the water. When she put the saucepan on the stove it hissed as if resentful and sent up a little white plume of steam.

There was a rumbling sound. Margret looked at her mother-in-law.

Granny laughed. "Not guilty," she said. "That was the Plattenberg."

Margret took a knife from the kitchen drawer and sat down at the table to help peel the potatoes. "Let's hope it's all over," she said.

"Yes," said Granny, "she isn't as young as she was."

Katharina pricked up her ears. What had she meant, not as young as she was? Mama was young, wasn't she? Young and strong and healthy?

"How long can you go on having children?" she asked,

and instantly regretted the question. It was almost as bad as asking how you died of a goitre. To her surprise, however, she got a straight answer.

"I was forty-six when I had Fridolin."

"And after that?"

"I didn't have any more."

The old woman fell silent. Katharina debated whether to ask the crucial question – Why didn't you have any more? – but she didn't dare. It was clear enough anyway: at 46 you were simply too old to have any more children and that was that. You probably couldn't stand the stress of all the pain and the puffing and blowing and sweating. Or should she ask all the same? She drew a deep breath. "When will Johannes and Fridolin be home?" she asked instead.

"Soon, I expect," said Granny. "They stop work earlier on Saturday afternoons."

Little Anna was discontented. She braced her feet against Katharina's thighs. Katharina turned her so that she could see her mother, who was sitting beside Granny and the heap of potatoes.

Margret waved to Anna, and the baby smiled and calmed down for a little while. Soon afterwards, when she started to whimper and kick, Margret took a potato and sent it rolling across the table. Katharina caught the potato and rolled it back to Margret, who said, "What's this, then?", and sent it back again. Anna went quiet at once, watching the process wide-eyed.

When the potato came rolling back yet again from

Katharina to Margret, Granny grabbed it and replaced it on the pile. "Food isn't for playing with," she said crossly.

Margret flushed, drew a deep breath, and sat up very straight. Anna waved her arms, staring at the pile of potatoes, and started fretting again.

"She was so nice and quiet just now," said Margret.

"You can always lay her down," said Granny, unmoved, and went on peeling potatoes. The mound of peelings grew, the pile of potatoes dwindled.

Two voices yodelled in the distance.

"That'll be them," said Granny. She went to get up but couldn't raise the energy.

"I'll go," said Margret. She opened the window and called back. Anna, who had quietened, stared at her mother and her grandmother in turn.

Katharina said she was going to look from the parlour. She handed Anna carefully to Margret, who came with her. Together they opened a window and looked down the track. Kaspar squeezed between them, but no one was in sight, so he went back to the doll's house.

"Those hens are still here," said Margret. Katharina caught sight of them strutting around among the red and yellow flowers. Then she looked back at the place where the track emerged from the trees.

"There they are!" she cried when the two brothers hove into view.

"Has the baby come?" Margret called.

"Not yet," Johannes called back. "But Kathrin's in labour and the midwife is with her."

Frightened by her mother's loud voice, Anna started crying. Katharina heard a nasty noise behind her and swung round: Kaspar had been sick into the doll's house.

12

"WHAT ARE THEY GOING TO CALL HIM?" ASKED PAUL. HE, Johannes, Fridolin, Granny, Margret and Katharina were sharing a big saucepan of potato mash at the kitchen table. Hans-Kaspar, who had just come in, was standing by the door with his jacket draped over one shoulder.

"'Him'?" he said with a laugh. "It's a girl. Born an hour ago."

Joyful cries rang out. Everyone spoke at once.

Katharina heard her grandmother say: "At last!" Margret asked: "Is she all right?" And Fridolin said: "I'm sure Schaaggli would have preferred a boy."

"Why?" That was Paul's voice. "He can always use another barmaid, especially if someone robs him of the one he's got!"

Loud laughter all round. Hans-Kaspar, blushing furiously, was invited to sit down. Paul got up and fetched the bottle and the little glasses from the kitchen cupboard. Once the glasses were filled, they all rose and toasted the newborn baby's health.

Katharina remained seated. In the momentary silence that followed while they all caught their breath after downing the potent schnapps, she asked: "What's her name?"

Hans-Kaspar hesitated. Nobody had mentioned that, he

said, they were so glad the baby had come at all. It must have been a difficult delivery, but Kathrin was all right. Her daughter Anna had already taken her a big jug of tea.

"Didn't they ever say what they were going to call the child?" asked Granny. The question was meant for her, Katharina realized, because every head had turned in her direction. She racked her brains. Then she remembered her father saying on one occasion that if it was a boy he would be called Samuel. A girl's name had never been mentioned.

She shook her head. The Samuel business needn't concern anyone. The baby was a girl, after all, and she was secretly pleased.

They ran through the members of the family. Anna had been named after Granny, Papa's mother; Regula after Mama's mother; Katharina after Mama herself. It was really the turn of Papa's grandmother, who was also the grandmother of Fridolin, Johannes and Paul – or, properly speaking, one of their two grandmothers. One had been called Euphemia and the other Verena. They quickly agreed on Euphemia. Euphemia was a very special name, said Granny, and her mother had been a very special person, a sturdy woman who had given birth to her younger brother Melchior in the morning and milked the cows in the stable that evening because her husband was late getting back from Glarus cattle market. The grown-ups promptly drank another toast to little Euphemia.

Katharina considered this a wholly unsuitable name for a newborn baby. That someone who had been on earth for only an hour should already be called Euphemia was quite unthinkable. Verena would suit a baby better. Besides, Mama and Papa would decide what her little sister was called, not their Bleiggen relations.

"Eat up before it gets cold," said Granny, and they all dug their forks into the yielding mass of potato, Hans-Kaspar included.

Katharina had lost her appetite but sipped a bowl of milk. She wondered if she would have to go back to the Meur tomorrow, but decided not to broach the subject as long as no one else did.

"Schaaggli said that Didi and the boy can come home again tomorrow," Hans-Kaspar added with his mouth full.

"We'll see," said Granny. "Kaspar was sick this afternoon."

"Right into the doll's house," said Katharina.

"Don't tell tales," Margret told her. "He couldn't help it."

Katharina hung her head. Why should telling the truth be telling tales? She'd had to clear up the mess, after all, and the very thought revolted her so much that she nearly brought up her potato mash. She fervently hoped that Kaspar was ill and that she might have to stay here until he was better. He was asleep for the moment. If only he wasn't sick into the bed tonight. Perhaps she should ask her grandmother's permission to sleep somewhere else? In the parlour, perhaps, either on the sofa or on the mattress on top of the stove. It would be lovely and warm up there, and she could take Lisi too. She certainly wouldn't forget her doll again, the way she had last night.

Uncle Paul's voice suddenly penetrated her consciousness.

Forester Seeli must be out of his mind, he said. Had he seriously demanded that the slate works remain closed until spring?

Hans-Kaspar was quick to add that the chairman of the district council had rejected that suggestion out of hand. Where else were a hundred men to find work?, the chairman had asked. Or so Hans-Kaspar had been told by young Elmer, who had overheard the conversation at the inn.

A hundred men . . . So many? Katharina had a mental image of them passing the Meur at dawn and dusk, their dusty boots and jackets as grey as the slate itself, particularly when they were returning home in the evening. They often walked in groups, and when a knot of men came tramping up from the iron bridge to Untertal their broad-brimmed hats made them look in the distance like walking mushrooms. Many of them stopped off at the Meur after work, especially on pay day. Then the talk would be of the slate quarry, of the dynamite they had detonated, of the exceptionally good slate they had come to, and of chisels that had got stuck or drill hammers lost. They would also give imitations of Foreman Müller, who was a German, spurring them on to greater effort or dressing them down if they failed to do something the way he wanted it done. One of his favourite phrases, which the quarrymen often repeated to the amusement of the whole taproom, was; "Safety supports? I don't see any safety supports, all I can see is first-class slate. Get it out!" Katharina had known those words by heart for ages but didn't know what they meant. Another thing she couldn't understand was why they all seemed so proud when something dangerous happened to them. To hear them talk, you'd think they were buried by scree or hit by stones every day, or that quarrymen had to be dragged from the rubble, half dead, after every blasting session. But that was men all over: they liked to exaggerate. Even so, she enjoyed listening to quarrymen's anecdotes rather than hunters' tales about shooting chamois and mountain goats. The quarrymen's stories sounded nearer the truth.

Katharina had seen a few of the younger workers in school last year. Though little older than her brother Jakob, they were already employed at the quarry – in fact some of them worked in the sheds as draughtsmen while still at school, marking out slabs of slate for the cutters. She recalled a taproom discussion in the course of which their neighbour Beat Rhyner had angrily thumped the table because parents sent their children out to work. A quarryman retorted that it was all very well for Beat to talk – he earned enough as a forester – but someone whose potatoes ran out in January took a different view of the matter.

Well, asked Paul, which was it to be? Would they close the quarry or carry on working? They would probably find out tomorrow, said Hans-Kaspar, when they collected their week's wages.

When Johannes asked about the trees on the Plattenberg, Hans-Kaspar described an argument between the two foresters. It seemed that Seeli had asked Marti to relieve the pressure on the slope by removing the timber, but Marti had said he wasn't going up there any more and wouldn't send anyone else, and if it was up to him he'd evacuate every house in Untertal and the occupants would have to get out fast. The others had jeered at him, apparently, and Heiri Elmer told him they were lucky that no one from Matt could tell the inhabitants of Elm when to shit their pants.

The kitchen rocked with laughter at this remark, and Paul raised his glass once more and toasted the mountain guide's quick wit. Then, noticing that Fridolin had left his glass untouched, he asked if he wasn't going to drink to Heiri.

Fridolin said he wasn't drinking to anyone. He didn't consider Marti a fool, even if he did come from Matt. Speaking for himself, he went on, he wouldn't go up there to fell trees for any money, not even ten francs a day. If Heiri Elmer and the council chairman were so sure it was safe, they were welcome to go up there together.

Katharina felt her heart beat faster. The hush that had descended on the kitchen resembled the silence that preceded a taproom brawl.

"So you think you know better than a district forester and a council chairman put together, do you?" said Paul, more slowly than usual, and glared at his youngest brother as if bent on nailing him to the wall with his eyes.

"No quarrelling, boys!" said Granny, banging the handle of her fork on the table.

That did the trick. The three brothers plunged their forks into the saucepan, Hans-Kaspar, Granny and Margret followed suit, and all that could be heard for a while were the sounds of chewing and swallowing.

Katharina's heart continued to pound. So one of the men who had been up there thought that Untertal should be evacuated. But Untertal wasn't just anywhere, it was where she lived – the inhabitants weren't just anyone, they were Mama and Papa and Anna and Regula and Jakob and Kaspar and herself, and the Rhyners and Old Jaggli and Young Jaggli, and old Elsbeth and young Elsbeth with the goitre, and all the children that went with them. Even her newborn sister was an inhabitant, whether her name was Euphemia or Verena, and they should all get out right away. She had a vision of the wagon swaying along the road to Matt, laden with all the possessions of the Martinsloch innkeeper and his family. She seemed to see it slowly disappearing down the valley accompanied by Fridolin, who was now sitting opposite her looking thoughtful; and she had a sudden feeling that he was the only one she could trust, and that the others knew nothing, least of all Uncle Paul with his jokes and jibes.

The silence in the kitchen told Katharina that the danger of an even bigger argument had still to be dispelled.

Granny turned to Johannes. "Did you find a use for Fridolin at the joiner's workshop?"

Johannes nodded. "Yes, indeed." Seeing that Paul was about to speak, he added: "Our stock of coffins is coming on nicely."

"Have you learnt anything about joinery?" Granny asked Fridolin.

He laughed. "Yes, the main thing I've learnt is how Johannes tests the finished articles."

"Well?"

"He lies in them himself."

13

"GENTLE JESUS, BE MY LIGHT, IN THE DARKNESS OF the night . . ."

Margret recited the prayer and Katharina softly said it with her, down to the concluding "Amen". She was lying in bed with her hands clasped together and the tips of her toes on the little bag of hot cherry stones. Kaspar, fast asleep beside her, was breathing deeply and peacefully. She had asked Margret whether she ought to wake him up and tell him he'd got a new baby sister, but Margret said it was better to leave him be. She felt his forehead and said she didn't think he was ill. If he had a good night's sleep they could certainly go back to the Meur tomorrow.

Kaspar had wanted a little brother, said Katharina, so he mightn't be pleased at all. In fact, she wasn't too sure that she really felt pleased herself. What gladdened her most was that her mother wouldn't have to lie in bed any more, panting and groaning with her hair all loose.

Margret had come upstairs to say prayers with her because Granny was too tired.

"Are you coming to bed too?" Katharina asked.

"No," said Margret, "I'm going back to the parlour for a bit."

"Margret?" Katharina whispered.

"Yes?" Margret paused in the doorway. The candle she'd left on the floor in the passage lit up her plaits like the sun going down behind a mountain ridge whose face is already in shadow. Katharina could hardly see her eyes.

"Could you leave the door open a crack?"

"If you like."

The door creaked as Margret pulled it to from the outside until only a thin strip of light seeped into the bedroom. The strip flickered, then faded by degrees as she descended the stairs. When she shut the kitchen door it was as dark as if the bedroom door were closed too.

Katharina was disappointed. She had hoped for a glimmer of light to go to sleep by.

But she did hear the others talking in the parlour. They said something to Margret as she went in, not that Katharina could make out what it was. She felt less frightened than she had last night. The spirits of the house seemed to be in a friendlier mood and meant her no harm. Perhaps they welcomed the birth of another human being – someone else to terrify later on.

The two hens were still awake, Katharina could hear them softly clucking in the front garden. Margret had failed to catch them, but they had only trampled a flower or two, so Granny had said to leave them there till someone came to claim them, be it only a fox.

Katharina thought of the neighbour she'd visited that morning on the hens' behalf. "Another mouth to feed . . ." Barbara's immediate reaction to the baby's birth had puzzled her until Granny explained that Barbara's husband had been crushed by a falling tree. That was two years ago, and the farm had been going downhill ever since. Joseph, Hans-Kaspar's brother, was too young to be much use, so it was better for Hans-Kaspar to go on working at the quarry. That way, at least someone brought a little money home to cover the bare necessities.

Katharina couldn't understand why God hadn't prevented the tree from falling on Barbara's husband; it wouldn't have been difficult, not for the Almighty. Or had the man committed some grave sin known only to God and been punished for it? But that would mean that Barbara and her children were being punished for something that wasn't their fault. Perhaps God wasn't just at all. Why else would he have let Afra Bäbler be struck by lightning? Looking for her goat, that was all Afra had been doing. Then Katharina suddenly thought how kind of God it was to have spared her mother and her little sister. Her hands were still clasped together, so she could offer up a quick word of thanks.

"Dear God," she prayed, "thank you for letting everything turn out all right."

Then she unclasped her hands and rolled over on her side, away from Kaspar. She slid her left arm under her head and knocked her wooden doll to the floor. "Poor Lisi," she said, "where have you got to?" – and shrank at the sound of her own voice. She leant out of bed as far as she could and felt around on the floor, but Lisi was nowhere to be found. Should she simply wait till tomorrow morning? Her flesh crawled at the thought of leaving her warm bed and groping around in the darkness beneath the bed. The doll was made of wood, after all; she could sleep on the wooden floorboards perfectly well. She might even have jumped out of bed because the idea appealed to her. Yes, that must be it, Katharina told herself. "Don't be afraid, Lisi," she whispered, "I'm here. Sleep well on the floorboards." Once again the sound of her own voice made her feel there was someone else in the room.

But the fear that had begun to steal over her was dispelled by voices raised in a hymn in the parlour downstairs. Katharina knew it: it was her grandmother's favourite from the old hymn book, the one everyone had to sing with her at New Year. Granny's voice was clearly audible. It always came in a little ahead of the men's deep voices, rather like the parson's when the congregation sang a hymn together in church. Katharina hoped she wouldn't be sent off to church tomorrow, not that anyone had mentioned it. She hadn't had to go to school, so she surely needn't go to Sunday school either. Anyway, Granny had already told her how the story of the Flood turned out. The problem of the fish was still unsolved, though, and it was a mystery that Noah had managed to get hold of marmots, chamois and mountain goats as well as monkeys, giraffes and elephants, considering how far apart they lived. Perhaps he'd caught some in advance in the Glarner Alps and taken them home with him. How did you catch a marmot? With a net? None of the hunters who drank at the Meur had ever talked of trapping animals, as far as she could remember, only of shooting them. She thought of the mousetraps Papa left in the storeroom. Before building the Ark, perhaps Noah had made some big traps for chamois and mountain goats and baited them with tasty herbs and left them in the mountains, and while waiting for the animals to walk into them he'd caught some marmots with a butterfly net like the one Schoolmaster Wyss owned. And then he'd loaded his haul on to a wagon and driven it back to the land of the Bible, so that when the Flood subsided there would be wild animals in the mountains once more.

Downstairs in the parlour the hymn had come to an end. Then Paul's voice made itself heard. He must have cracked a joke, because everyone laughed. They struck up another song, not a hymn this time, but "Up On the Mountain", each verse of which ended with the words "and never was seen again".

Katharina liked that song. Although she had never worked out who or what was never seen again, she suspected some connection with what people got up to behind the house at night when they were old enough to do so. There was also something about the dairyman laying aside his milking pail and dancing with the milkmaid. If they danced together, it certainly wouldn't be long before they disappeared behind the cowshed for a kiss – unless they kissed in the cowshed itself when no one was looking.

It would soon be time for the annual fair, when people sang, danced and made music in the Meur until late at night. Katharina was looking forward to that. Last year she had helped to decorate the dance hall. There was a whole chest filled with coloured paper chains, and she and Regula had draped them over the antlers hanging on the walls. That evening the band turned up complete with accordion and clarinet, and the man who played the bass fiddle had even let her pluck the strings – it astonished her that she could produce such deep notes. And the young men of the village appeared with flowers and feathers in their hats, looking quite different from the way they looked when going to work at the slate quarry. Each of them paid one franc and was handed a sprig of rosemary as proof of payment, the sprigs having been bound with twine by Katharina and Regula on instructions from Hans-Kaspar. He was among the youngsters who brought the band and ordered the food, which usually made the whole inn smell of chamois stew and marmot fat. The girls were a specially fine sight in their voluminous pleated skirts, which whirled around so gaily when they danced. They too were adorned with flowers woven into their plaits, but the most important flower was the carnation at their breast: if it pointed downwards the girl had no boy to go behind the house with; if it pointed upwards she already had one.

The song about the dairyman and the milkmaid came to an end. It was Fridolin who struck up the next one, this time about the flea that went to Alsace to fetch a cask of wine.

Katharina liked that song too. She didn't know where Alsace was, admittedly, but it must have plenty of everything. She remembered her father saying, only a few days ago, that if it went on raining like this the potatoes would rot again and they'd have to send for some from Alsace, like last year. There were plenty of potatoes there, that much was clear; but as for the cows in Alsace walking on stilts and the donkeys on tightropes and the goats wearing boots – that was just a joke, it only happened in the song. And the flea liked Alsace so much that it bought a house there and never came back. Perhaps they should all move to Alsace – Papa, Mama, Anna, Jakob, Regula, herself, Kaspar, and the new-born baby – and buy a house next door to the flea's. Then they could all watch the cows walk on stilts, and Lobe, her own cow, would end up getting the knack of it, and so would Bless and Stern, who were still out to pasture on the Falzüber Alp; and people would have to use stilts themselves in order to milk them. And suddenly she was in Alsace and the donkey on the tightrope was holding the stilts for her, and she hopped light-footedly along the tightrope to the donkey, which waved to her as it stood poised in the middle, and she mounted the stilts and the donkey handed her the milking pail; but Joseph, the lazy brute, laid aside his pail and danced with a milkmaid in red boots and a pleated skirt that whirled around; but it wasn't a milkmaid at all, it was a goat with a snapped carnation hanging downwards in its muzzle, and the goat bent its glassy gaze on the mountain and stamped on the ground so hard that the antlers in the houses fell off the walls and the window panes rattled and the cows' skulls over the barn doors hung awry.

14

WHEN KATHARINA GOT OUT OF BED TO SIT ON THE chamber pot she trod on something hard and gave a startled little cry. By the dim light filtering through the cracks in the shutters she saw that the object beneath her heel was her wooden doll. Having used the pot, she pushed it back under the bed, picked up Lisi, and crept beneath the warm bedclothes once more. Beside her, Kaspar stirred and sat up.

"Want to wee," he said.

Reluctantly, she wriggled out from between the sheets, walked round the bed, and pulled out his chamber pot.

"Come on," she said, lifting the bedclothes and holding out her hand.

He went on weeing for such a long time, she was afraid the pot would overflow.

"Finished," he said at last. He stood up and climbed back into bed.

Katharina pushed the pot back under the bed with some distaste. "We've got a little sister," she said.

"Where?"

"Down at the Meur. At home."

"Not a little brother?"

"No, a little sister."

Kaspar didn't speak for a while. Then he said: "Want a drink of water."

Katharina sighed. She'd been about to get back into bed. "Can't you wait? It'll be breakfast time soon."

"I'm thirsty."

It occurred to her that he might be ill – he'd been sick yesterday.

"Wait," she said. "I'll go down to the kitchen."

The bedroom door was still ajar. She pushed it open and tiptoed down the stairs, hearing them creak a little. The deserted kitchen looked strangely unfamiliar in the half light of dawn. A smell of cold potatoes and herb schnapps hung in the air. Last night's dirty plates lay on the draining board beside the sink, saucepan and all. Obviously no one had bothered to wash up.

Katharina dipped her finger in the big tub. The water was lukewarm, which meant she would have to get some fresh from the fountain outside. She took a drinking bowl from the shelf and she went out into the hall. There she pulled on her shoes with the laces stuffed inside; she could feel them against the soles of her feet. Was the front door locked? No. She lifted the heavy latch and pulled.

She couldn't believe her eyes: no sooner had the door opened a crack than Züsi, the cat from the Meur, slipped through it and rubbed against her legs, mewing.

"Züsi!" she said softly. "What are you doing up here?"

Squatting down with the bowl in one hand, she stroked the cat with the other. It was Züsi, all right. There was no mistaking her tabby cat with the black paws and the white fleck behind one ear.

She could hear Kaspar yammering upstairs. How could anyone manage to call loudly and quietly at the same time? "I'm coming," she hissed up the stairwell. She rose to her feet. "Wait here," she told the cat.

Nero growled as she crossed the forecourt to the fountain, but her "Quiet, damn you!" was an immediate success. Having filled the bowl, she cautiously returned to the house, deposited the bowl on the little bench in the hall, removed her shoes, and climbed the stairs with the cat at her heels.

Kaspar was sitting bolt upright in bed, waiting for her impatiently. Just as she went to hand him the bowl he caught sight of the cat.

"Züsi?" he asked in astonishment.

"Yes," said Katharina. "She's come to pay us a visit . . . drink up!" she added, thrusting the bowl at him when he went on staring at the cat. After all, she'd gone out into the cold for his sake.

Kaspar gulped the water down without taking his eyes off the cat, which continued to wind itself around Katharina's legs. "Finished," he said at length.

No one else in the house was stirring, so Katharina crept back under the covers. Züsi was up on the bed in a trice. She lay down at the foot on Katharina's side and curled up into a ball, purring.

Kaspar giggled. "Züsi's come to bed."

"She's sleepy like us," Katharina told him. "It's too early to get up."

She turned away from him and stuck her thumb in her mouth. She never sucked her thumb at home if anyone was looking; thumb-sucking earned her a slap on the hand from her parents or the older children if they caught her at it. No one could tell her off now, though. Lisi was snuggled up beside her and Züsi was lying at the foot of the bed. The thumb in her mouth was like the cheese in the fairy tale, which never got any smaller, and it made her mouth go all juicy. Things couldn't be nicer, she thought suddenly, and the nicest thing of all would be to lie here like this for the rest of her life.

There was a rumble in the distance.

Granny could be heard yawning loudly in the bedroom downstairs, and her bed creaked.

Was that Uncle Paul getting up in the room next door, or was he merely using the pot, like her and Kaspar, before going back to bed? Today was Sunday and people didn't have to get up as early as they did on weekdays. But Blüemli, who didn't know it was Sunday, had to be milked just the same. On the other hand, a cow didn't have to go to church. Katharina tried to imagine what it would be like if all the villagers' cows came to church and assembled on the gravel forecourt outside the big door, mooing, or roamed around between the graves in the churchyard, munching the flowers and grass. Perhaps they would want to join in thanking Noah for saving them from the Great Flood, and the other animals would come too, the goats and sheep, hens and ibexes, chamois and marmots and foxes, but not the fish, which had survived without Noah's help. There would be a terrible crush and the congregation wouldn't know what to do, nor would Parson Mohr. Perhaps he would try to lead them in a psalm – "I will lift up mine eyes unto the hills" – and the cows would low, and the goats and sheep would bleat, and the hens would cluck, and the marmots would whistle through their teeth, and the chamois and ibexes would blow through their nostrils, and the foxes would bark hoarsely and leer at the hens, and Schoolmaster Wyss would finger the keys of the organ while Siegrist sweated as he pumped the bellows, and Noah, who would surely be rejoicing in heaven, would summon the Almighty and his son and point down at Elm so that the two of them had something to laugh at for once.

Then the dogs joined in and the cats began to mew, and Katharina woke up. Margret was standing in the doorway with Anna on her hip and Kaspar's hand in hers, staring in surprise at Züsi, who was stretching luxuriously and regarding the figures in the doorway like a queen surveying her subjects. Kaspar, highly amused, looked from Züsi to Margret and back again.

"Where did the cat come from?" Margret asked.

Katharina told her that Züsi had been waiting outside the front door at dawn, when she went to fetch some water from the fountain.

Margret shook her head. Nothing of the kind had ever happened before, she said. What had possessed the animal, and how had it found its way up the mountain? There was bread and milk in the kitchen, and Katharina mustn't forget to empty the pots and bring them upstairs again.

116

Then she went down to the kitchen with Kaspar and Anna. Katharina got up, opened the windows, and pushed the shutters back.

No sun again today, just grey clouds wherever you looked, and grass, trees and flowers glistening with moisture. Three crows were chasing a bird of prey over the trees, cawing harshly. In the front garden the two white hens clucked as they busily strutted back and forth between the flower beds and the rhubarb patch.

A flock of sparrows flew up from the track and out of sight. They must have landed on the roof, because a moment later the whole house seemed to come alive with their twittering.

Silenced briefly by another rumble from the Plattenberg, the birds soon chirped away even louder than before.

This time Katharina spotted the place where the rock had broken off. In the distance, above the highest treetops, she saw a little cloud of dust rising from a raw grey patch in the midst of the dark green firs. She couldn't see which way the rock had fallen, of course, but there was only one possible direction and that was downwards; and down below the Plattenberg, she knew, lay the slate works and, just beyond them, the Meur.

"Didi!" called a voice from the kitchen.

"Coming!" she called back.

She wasn't even dressed yet, and what about the chamber pots? Today was Sunday, so perhaps she ought to wear her Sunday frock. But that was probably still hanging in the parlour or stowed away in some cupboard or other. She put on her grey knitted jacket over her nightshirt and went to the door. Then, not wanting another scolding from Margret, she retraced her steps and gingerly extracted the two pots from under the bed. She carefully descended the stairs and made her way along the passage to the lavatory. The door was locked, and she could hear someone groaning in travail with a Fat Aunt. The struggle terminated in a sigh of relief, and Johannes finally emerged in a cloud of evil-smelling air.

"Well, well, if it isn't little Didi," he said. "All right – give me those potties."

He took them from her, tipped them down the lavatory, and handed them back. Noticing that she was about to put her shoes on, he said the pots were clean enough and didn't need rinsing at the fountain. Katharina flitted upstairs, replaced them under the bed, and hurried back downstairs to the kitchen, where all the others were seated at the table in front of their bowls of coffee or milk. In the middle lay a big loaf of bread from which several slices had been cut.

"Here comes our sleepyhead," Paul said with a laugh, and Granny asked Katharina if she would like some milk. She blushed and nodded, and when the delicious white milk flowed from the pitcher into her bowl and Fridolin passed her a slice of bread that smelt of Sunday she slowly began to believe that it might, after all, turn out to be a nice day.

15

KATHARINA WAS STANDING ON A KITCHEN STOOL AT THE
sink, trying to scrub the crust off the bottom of the saucepan
with a brush. She had already washed up all the plates and
bowls and put them on the draining board beside the sink.
The first plate was propped against a bowl and the second
plate against the first, and so on, with the result that they
all leaned sideways like a file of Suvorov's soldiers bracing
themselves against the wind.

"That'll make a nice little job for Didi," Granny had said.
Katharina deeply mistrusted that turn of phrase because the
little job in question nearly always turned out to be a big and
exceptionally strenuous one.

Her father had called it "a little job" when he sent her into
one of the two big wine casks that stood in the cellar of the
Meur. When one of them was empty, she would open a small
trapdoor above the spigot that was just big enough to admit
a child her size. Then she had to crawl inside and scour the
bottom and sides of the barrel with a scrubbing brush and
a swab while Papa lit the interior with his storm lantern. The
casks were big enough for her to stand up in. When she
remembered how her father came down the cellar stairs
with her and how he hoisted her up a little to enable her to

crawl inside, and how he remained with her the whole time, ready to wring out the wine-sodden floor-cloth whenever she handed it to him, and how he stuck his head through the little doorway to point out places where the tartar deposit hadn't been completely removed, and how he lifted her down when she'd finished and gave her a whole handful of dried pear slices, which he produced from his trouser pocket in the cellar itself – when she remembered all these things, she realised she was already looking forward to cleaning out the next wine cask even though she also had a horrific recollection of the time the lantern went out and Papa hadn't any matches with him and had to go upstairs to fetch some, leaving her all alone in the dark cellar, in the bowels of an even darker wine cask, enveloped in a sweetish-squash-smelling murk that threatened to asphyxiate her. Down on her knees with her head poking out of the little trapdoor, she'd started to cry loudly and violently – almost bellowing – and when the wavering light of the lantern returned she'd insisted on climbing out of the cask right away, and Papa had to hold her in his arms and talk to her in a coaxing way before she crawled in again to complete the "little job". And she well remembered how Papa had comforted her, telling her that only she, Katharina, could manage it because Jakob and Regula were already too big for the little trapdoor, and how glad of her help he was because he didn't know how he would have got the cask clean otherwise.

She had never before heard him say he was glad of her help, and Mama had never said such a thing either, not even when she sent her to fetch eggs from old Elsbeth.

Anyway, why should parents be glad of their children? Children simply existed; they came into being in the mysterious way Katharina planned to ask her eldest sister about the next time they were alone together. Mama certainly hadn't seemed glad of her when she lay in bed with clammy hands, groaning.

But Mama was bound to be feeling better again by now. She must have drunk plenty of tea and slept for a long time, except when the baby woke her because it was thirsty. So Mama would also have to hold a baby to her breast like Kleophea and Margret. Katharina had never seen her mother's breasts, but she was looking forward to the sight quite as eagerly as she was to the sight of her new little sister.

Women had two breasts, which was a practical arrangement if they had twins. "A mother has two breasts and gives birth to twins. How many breasts per child does that make?" Katharina giggled. No sum like that would ever appear in their arithmetic book, but why not? Why not in the chapter headed "The Numerals One and Two"? There were all kinds of sums about fathers, like the really childishly easy one that went: "A father wishes to divide two apples between his two children. How many apples does each child get?" Anna Elmer had actually answered: "Two." Katharina remembered that only too well, largely because Anna had had to hold out her hands and get a slap on each from Herr Wyss, making two slaps in all.

She could hear Kaspar mooing in the parlour. Granny had let him play with the doll's house again, although he'd been sick into it only yesterday, and he didn't even have to help her in the kitchen. He was obviously herding the animals into their stable, because he bleated like a sheep and barked like a dog in quick succession. Katharina felt indignant. She wanted to play with the doll's house too. It was Sunday, after all, so why should she of all people be stuck in the kitchen when none of the grown-ups was working? The burnt potato on the bottom of the saucepan was incredibly hard to shift, far harder than the tartar on a wine cask, and she'd added not only a dash of vinegar but a spoonful of sand from the can beside the sink. She got down off her stool, carried it over to the kitchen range, and took the salt jar from the overhead shelf. Reaching into it, she extracted as much as salt as she could pick up between her thumb and three fingers, deposited the jar on the range, returned to the sink, and crumbled the salt into the saucepan. Then she retrieved her stool, mounted it again, and proceeded to scrub as hard as she could. It was a trick copied from her sister Anna, whose maxim on such occasions was: "If sand doesn't shift it, try salt."

Still, she was glad she didn't have to go to church. Kleophea's baby was being christened today, so the service would be longer than usual, and Granny had already told her the story of Noah, which Parson Mohr would be recounting in Sunday school. "Meer" meant sea, so had the Meer Glacier got its name from the Flood? The glacier itself would have been submerged by the sea, and so would the Hausstock. That meant fish must have swum above the pastures on the Bleiggen, not to mention the Meur, which would have lain, unimaginably far below the surface, on the seabed.

There was a rumble from outside. Züsi crept under the stool and started mewing. Katharina glanced at the bowl of bread and milk that Margret had prepared for the cat and left beside the stove. It was still untouched. She got down off the stool, fetched the bowl and put it on the floor beside the sink. "Go on," she told the cat, "that's all you're getting." The two yellow eyes stared at her reproachfully, the mewing persisted. Katharina took hold of Züsi's head and rammed it into the bowl. Indignantly, the cat wriggled free and fled through the door into the parlour.

"Suit yourself," said Katharina, and mounted her stool again. Just as she picked up the brush she heard a sharp, vicious noise from the kitchen range: the salt jar had cracked in half, the contents were trickling out and starting to smoke. She jumped down, knocking over the stool and jogging the cat's bowl. Milk slopped over the rim and meandered across the kitchen floor.

Katharina was in despair. "Granny!" she called, pushing the parlour door open. "Granny!"

Kaspar, who was crouching in front of the doll's house with two miniature sheep in his hand, looked up in surprise. An instant later Granny emerged into the parlour from her bedroom followed by Margret, who was holding one of her plaits. The rest of Granny's hair hung loose down her back.

"Good heavens, child, what's the matter?"

"In the kitchen!" cried Katharina. She returned to the

range, which was giving off a strangely acrid smell of scorched salt.

With a sigh, the two women set about cleaning up the mess. Granny removed the broken glass from the range and swept the hotplate with a dustpan and brush, adding a smell of singed horsehair to that of scorched salt. Margret picked up the cat's bowl, which had also broken in two, and put it on the table. Katharina had to collect the morsels of bread on a plate and tip them into the pigswill bucket that stood in the hall. Margret used a floorcloth to mop up the milk and wrung it out into the saucepan.

They might have rehearsed it, everything went so quickly, and it wasn't until the whole room was neat and tidy again that Granny asked Katharina what on earth had induced her to put the salt jar on the range. Close to tears, Katharina told her about the sand-and-salt trick. It hadn't occurred to her, of course, that the hotplate would still be hot.

"Idiot," said Margret, tweaking her ear so hard that she yelped, but Granny said it could have been worse. "Glass and luck are brittle muck," she added, drawing on her store of homely proverbs.

Kaspar stared at the two halves of the cat's bowl and said: "Broken."

"We know," Katharina told him defiantly. "Get back to your doll's house."

It might be possible to glue them together, said Granny. Johannes was good at such things, he could try this evening. Then she asked Katharina if she'd like to accompany the three men to church and go on home from there, but that was the last thing Katharina wanted to do, even if she had to wash up the lunch things as well. She would finish scouring the potato saucepan, she said, hastily pushing the stool back in front of the sink.

No, said Granny, never mind, she'd already been a hard-working girl and washed up all the dishes. Margret could finish off the saucepan. Perhaps it was a bit too hard for little Kathrinli to manage.

Margret gave Katharina a resentful look as she picked up the scouring brush. Katharina felt stung, not only by Margret's expression but by Granny's "little Kathrinli". When Granny suggested walking down to the Meur together that afternoon, she said: "Why?"

There was a moment's silence in the kitchen. The sparrows chirped on the roof as if intent on driving away some great, universal foe. Margret lowered the brush and turned to stare at her. Granny looked puzzled.

"Why not?" she asked.

16

"COME ON, CHICKABIDDY," CALLED KASPAR. HE TOOK
a handful of breadcrumbs from the bowl and threw them
at the hens in the front garden. Katharina was holding
him up a little so that he could reach over the fence. Behind
them stood Margret, who had come to see how the stray
birds were doing.

Cautiously, at first, the strays emerged from under the
rhubarb leaves and made their way along the little path
between the two beds of red and yellow flowers to where
the breadcrumbs had landed. Kaspar promptly followed
up the first handful with a second.

Katharina let her brother slide to the ground, and together
they watched the birds peck up the bread. At least they
hadn't gone hungry or been taken by a fox, Margret said.
The person who'd lost them would probably turn up sometime; the menfolk might have heard something after church
today. Otherwise, she said with a laugh – otherwise they'd
at least have next week's Sunday lunch. It wasn't every day
your Sunday roast walked into the house of its own accord.

"Almost like in Alsace, isn't it?" said Katharina, proud of
having made a little joke.

"How do you mean?" asked Margret.

Katharina was disappointed. Margret hadn't understood, even though she was a grown-up.

"You know, like the song you sang last night, where everything's topsy-turvy." She waited for Margret to laugh at the joke now that she'd had it explained to her.

But Margret merely gave a little nod and said: "Oh, *that's* what you meant."

There was a rattle like gunfire from the Plattenberg. The hens froze for a moment, then went on eating. Margret and Katharina turned and tried to find the place where the rocks had broken off, but they couldn't see it.

"Want to go indoors," said Kaspar.

"No need to be scared," Katharina told him. "We're at Granny's."

A yodel could be heard from the wood below the house.

Margret yodelled back. "Paul's coming," she said, her eyes sparkling.

Katharina thought how nice it was to be a grown-up. You were worried, but your husband simply yodelled to you from the wood and came home, and all was well.

She shared Margret's pleasure when her husband came walking up the track through the trees with Fridolin at his side, both wearing dark hats. Wasn't Johannes coming too? Yes, there he was, also wearing a hat; but following him were the hatless figures of a man and a woman. Katharina recognised them both: the man was Hans-Kaspar from the house up the hill, the woman her elder sister Anna.

"Anna's coming!" cried Katharina, and hurried down the track to meet the new arrivals.

"How are you, Didi?" asked Anna, taking her hand. Hans-Kaspar was walking close beside her, and Katharina thought she'd spotted her letting go of his hand a moment earlier.

"I'm fine," she said. She released Anna's hand, then turned and took hold of it again so as to walk up to the house beside her.

"And Kaspar?"

"He's fine again too."

"Again? What do you mean?"

"He was sick yesterday," said Katharina. Into the doll's house, she was about to add, but remembered Margret's reprimand just in time and changed her mind.

Kaspar had come running towards them in Katharina's wake, but before he could greet his eldest sister, Paul cut him off and picked him up. "Got you!" he cried, holding the little boy above his head.

Kaspar kicked and struggled, crowing with laughter. Then Paul turned and put him down at Anna's feet. "Someone else wants to welcome you," he said. Kaspar promptly insinuated himself between Anna and her beau and reached for her free hand, which she willingly gave him.

Margret had now come down the track. "What about me?" she asked Paul with a smile.

He grabbed her by the hips, two-handed, and hoisted her into the air as quickly and easily as if she were a bale of hay. Margret shrieked at him to put her down but he wouldn't. "You wanted to fly, so you must stay up there," he told her.

Kaspar chuckled delightedly. "Margret's flying," he said to Anna and Katharina and himself.

"Yes," said Paul, "Margret's flying home." And he carried his shrieking, kicking wife up the steep path to the front garden, going redder and redder in the face as he did so.

To Katharina it looked as if a huge bird was fluttering above Paul's hat – as if Noah were capturing one of his brace of vultures.

Fridolin and Johannes egged their brother on. "Put her in with the hens," yelled Fridolin.

"Where the womenfolk belong," Johannes called after him.

"And where do *you* belong?" Anna interjected.

Fridolin laughed. "With the pigs!"

"Here we are." Panting, Paul dumped his wife on the grass in front of the garden fence and kissed her on the cheek. "You didn't know your husband was such a muscle man, did you?"

Margret, who didn't know whether to be angry or pleased, decided on the latter. She couldn't bring herself to sulk – everyone was in such a cheerful, exuberant mood.

"Just don't pass out on me," she told Paul, whose chest was still heaving, "or I'll have to carry you indoors."

Paul laughed, then turned to Anna. "See?" he said. "There are those hens of yours."

Katharina looked surprised. "You mean they're ours?"

"No," said Anna, "they belong to old Elsbeth. She's been looking everywhere for them. I'll take them down to her right away. You and Kaspar can come too. Papa and Mama and your baby sister are expecting you."

Katharina frowned. She didn't want to go back home so

soon. It might be true that their parents were expecting them, but it seemed unlikely that the same applied to their newborn sister, who didn't even know them.

"Are they really the ones?" Margret asked Anna. She indicated the hens, which were warily retreating towards the house.

"They could be," said Anna. "One of them's supposed to have a brownish patch on the backside."

"Comes of not wiping itself properly," quipped Paul, provoking a chorus of male laughter.

"The one on the right has, do you see?" Margret called, pointing to the hen in question, which was disappearing into the flowers. "Catching them, that's the only problem."

Anna opened the garden gate and took a few cautious steps along the front of the house. "Where have they got to?" she asked in a low voice.

"There!" called Granny. She was leaning out of the window.

Startled, the hens fluttered into the air and tried to escape over the fence. Katharina screamed and buried her face in her arms because one of them flew straight at her. Johannes intercepted the bird, grabbed it by the legs, and held it upside down. The hen resisted, furiously flapping its wings, one of which brushed Katharina. She stepped back so abruptly that Kaspar, who was just behind her, fell over.

The second hen hadn't managed to clear the fence. It flopped back into the front garden and ran along the fence, panic-stricken, with Anna in hot pursuit. Being reluctant to trample on the flowers, however, she failed to catch it. Then

Hans-Kaspar threw a stone and hit it on the head. The bird staggered and stopped short, whereupon Anna deftly caught it by the legs and held it upside down above her head.

The hens' indignant squawks, the calls for string to tie their legs with, the sobs emitted by Kaspar, who had rolled a little way down the slope, the men's triumphant shouts, the women's laughter – all these combined to produce a sound that almost dazed Katharina and at the same time filled her with happiness, almost like the singing last night. She tried to help Kaspar up, but he angrily snatched his hand away when she took it and scrambled to his feet unaided.

All he said was: "Silly cow!"

"Moo!" Katharina retorted, putting out her tongue at him.

The hens, their legs lashed together with lengths of string which Granny threw out of the window, were hung on a fence post. Their clucking gradually quietened, as if they'd accepted that their fate.

"Well," asked Granny from the window, "how was it in church? Was the Nigg baby christened?"

"I suppose so," said Fridolin.

Granny looked puzzled. "What do you mean?"

"You could hardly hear a thing, the rockfalls were making such a din. Parson Mohr even sent Siegrist out in the middle of a hymn to see what had happened. Another load came down just when he got to the christening, then everyone ran outside. Some of the rocks had come to rest a few feet short of the Martinsloch, in fact one of them only just missed the place. It's lying in the middle of the Raminer – the water's already backing up."

"A few more," Paul said with a grin, "and there'll be a lake behind the Meur!"

"What about Kathrin and the baby?" Granny asked Anna.

"They're fine. Mama lost quite a lot of blood, though, so she's still very weak. She hadn't got up by the time I left, but there's nothing wrong with the baby. It's feeding well."

"Thank God," said Granny.

"Are the children ready to leave?" Anna asked.

"No," said Katharina, "I'd rather have lunch up here." A promising aroma was drifting out of the window. It smelt almost like New Year's Day.

Anna declined an invitation to stay for lunch because she was needed down at the Meur. Granny said she would bring the children home that afternoon and told her to pick some dahlias for Kathrin.

Just then the cat appeared on the window sill.

"Züsi, you wandering gypsy!" cried Anna. "Are you coming home with me and the hens?"

Züsi rubbed against Granny's elbow, purring. "I'll bring her when I come with the children," said Granny.

Anna said that no one in Untertal could work out how the cat had found its way up to the Bleiggen, and the business of the hens was equally mysterious.

"Animals have their moods too," Paul said. "Just like children, eh, Didi?" And he gave Katharina a slap on the shoulder that almost knocked her down.

"Yes," said Katharina. "Perhaps they're scared," she added quickly.

Nonplussed by her reply, everyone lapsed into silence. Then

132

Granny said that those who were staying must come inside. The food would be on the table any minute.

Moments later, when only Katharina, Hans-Kaspar and Anna were still outside the house, Hans-Kaspar said he would look in at the Meur again that evening. It began to rain. Anna set off down the hill, clutching a bunch of red dahlias and carrying the softly clucking hens by the string around their legs. When she turned before entering the trees and gave an awkward final wave, the lump in Katharina's throat felt bigger than the goitre that had killed her grandfather.

17

"NO," SAID KATHARINA.

Granny had just asked her to get ready to accompany her and Kaspar down to the Meur. Kneeling beside the doll's house in the parlour, Katharina had assembled the entire family of bones in front of it. They were all standing in a row: the farmer, the farmer's wife, the farmhand, the milk-maid, and three children. She was in the process of removing the two cows from the cowshed and adding them to the sheep, pigs and dog at the end of the row. The poultry she'd previously installed on top of the stove, where her grand-mother had taken a brief nap on the mattress before going to her bedroom to get changed for the visit to Untertal. The only way you could reach the mattress was by climbing three high steps behind the stove, and Katharina had carried each of the six bone hens up there one by one. When Kaspar asked where the chickabiddies were going, she had answered: "Up to the Bleiggen." The farmer and his family had now decided to join the hens, and everyone else was coming too, animals included, because they insisted on knowing where the hens had got to.

"But child," said Granny, "don't you want to see your baby sister?"

"No."

Katharina removed the second cow from its stall and put it with the first, which was already standing between a pig and the dog.

"Why not?"

"I'll be a nursemaid long enough."

Her mother had told her more than once how much she was counting on her help when the baby was born.

Granny shook her head. "Now listen," she said, "you're to help Kaspar on with his shoes and cape – and put your own on too while you're at it. And get your bundle ready. Margret can help you."

Reluctantly, Katharina took Kaspar's hand and went out through the kitchen into the hall. Her nostrils were pleasantly assailed by the scent of ham and cabbage that lingered over the table where they had all been seated not long before, reminding her of the wonderful meal that lay, warm and comforting, in her stomach. The men had spent almost the whole of lunch-time arguing about the same thing, namely whether such a rockfall in the middle of a church service meant anything, and whether work at the quarry should be stopped, and who should decide the issue anyway, a forester from Glarus or a forester from Matt or the inhabitants of Elm themselves. And when Paul loudly poured scorn on "a few little stones", Fridolin cocked his curly head and kept saying they shouldn't forget, they must also bear in mind, they ought to consider what might happen. And Johannes nodded at each of them in turn and looked rather unhappy, because he would much have preferred to eat in silence. The women seemed to have no opinion on the matter, which Katharina found puzzling. Margret said nothing and Granny occasionally said they shouldn't quarrel on a Sunday and asked who wanted some more ham or cabbage. Whenever Fridolin spoke Katharina lowered her fork and stopped chewing, and when Paul took the floor she looked at her plate and went on eating.

Afterwards, with peace restored, they all set off for the village. Fridolin planned to collect his week's wages from the slate works, Johannes was bound for the inn, and Paul had to see the shingle-maker in Steinibach because the stable roof needed repairing.

Katharina knelt down in front of Kaspar, who was seated on the little bench in the hall, and slipped one of his shoes on. Just as she picked up the other one she heard the cat mewing. Züsi was standing in the kitchen doorway, rubbing her back against the doorpost.

Katharina dropped the second shoe and went through the kitchen and parlour to her grandmother's bedroom. "Granny?" she said from the doorway.

Her grandmother was sitting on a chair with a jewel box open on her lap. Katharina promptly forgot what she'd meant to ask her and stared in wonder at the little casket's glittering contents. She could see necklaces and bracelets and brooches, and wasn't that a string of pearls hanging over the edge? Where was she, in Granny's bedroom or the Emperor of China's palace?

"This," said Granny, holding up a brooch, "is for little Euphemia. It belonged to my grandmother. Do you like it?"

136

Katharina came closer, and Granny put the brooch in her hand. It was shaped like a dainty silver flower.

Katharina nodded. Of course she liked it. She couldn't imagine anyone not liking such a brooch.

"Every grandchild gets a little piece of jewellery from me at birth. You've got one too, haven't you?"

It occurred to Katharina that her mother was keeping a barrette for her. "Yes," she said, "but I'm not allowed to wear it until I'm confirmed."

"You'll be old enough to take care of it then. Afterwards, you'll have it all your life."

Katharina felt she was already old enough to take care of a hair clasp, but she refrained from saying so.

Granny wrapped the brooch in a piece of tissue paper. She was shutting the jewel box when Kaspar appeared with a shoe in his hand.

"Shoe," he said reproachfully.

"Yes," said Granny, "get a move on."

Katharina suddenly remembered what she'd meant to ask.

"Granny," she said, "what do we do about Züsi?"

Her grandmother said she'd fetch the lidded basket from the kitchen right away, if Katharina would catch the cat and bring it to her.

Kaspar was delighted to hear this. "Catch Züsi!" he yelled. He ran to the kitchen door with his shoe in his hand and hurled it at the cat, which promptly scampered up the stairs.

"Don't be so silly," Katharina shouted at him. "You'll scare her away like that!"

Undeterred, Kaspar clambered up the stairs, but his

enthusiasm waned a little when the cat hissed at him from the landing. He paused and looked back at his sister, who squeezed past and tried some friendly persuasion. "Come here, Züsi," she said, as ingratiatingly as she could. "Come on, you can go home now."

But it seemed that Züsi didn't feel like going home, because she fled up the stairs leading to the top floor, where Johannes and Fridolin slept. Katharina had never been up there before, and it was only with some hesitation that she put her foot on the bottom step. "Now she's gone all the way up," she snarled at Kaspar, who was also in the passage now.

"Here, children," Granny called from below. "Get ready first. The cat will come down of its own accord."

Whimpering sounds began to issue from Margret's room. The door opened and Margret peered out. "What's all the rumpus?" she demanded angrily. "You've woken the baby." Looking sheepish, Katharina and Kaspar slunk past her and went downstairs again. Granny sat Kaspar on the little bench, manœuvred his foot into the shoe he'd thrown at Züsi, and tied his laces. Katharina felt relieved at this because she could only tie her own easily. In order to tie Kaspar's she had to stand behind him so the laces were in front of her like her own. And if Kaspar, who thoroughly disliked this procedure, turned round, it spoilt the whole thing and she had to start again from scratch.

"Well, Didi, what about *your* shoes?" asked Granny.

Katharina, who was still in her socks, realised she'd been standing there watching as if she weren't going with them. She hadn't put her cape on, nor had she packed her bundle.

138

"I'm not coming," she said. Instantly, the blood rushed to her head. *What* had she said?

It was completely out of order. She was still a little girl, so little that they wouldn't even give her the hair clasp that belonged to her, and her grandmother was a grown-up; you simply didn't talk to her that way. Somehow, though, it was as if she herself hadn't said it, but another Katharina had – one who dwelt somewhere inside her.

"*What* was that?" Granny said quickly, and Katharina, who had really meant to say she would put her shoes on at once, repeated the forbidden sentence: "I'm not coming."

She hung her head in the certainty that she would get a slap or, at the very least, that her grandmother would pull her plaits. Instead, Granny said something quite unexpected: "So when *do* you want to go home?"

Katharina hadn't given the matter any thought, but her other self stepped in once more – the answer seemed to slip out of its own accord. "After school tomorrow. I could go straight to school from here, couldn't I?"

Granny said nothing, so she added: "I know the way, after all."

And when Granny still said nothing, the other Katharina said briskly: "I could walk down to school with Barbara's Lena."

The longer the silence persisted, the smaller her grown-up grandmother and the bigger the other Katharina seemed to become.

"Stubborn little monkey," said Granny.

The two Katharinas exulted in silence. They knew they'd won.

"You get your stubborn streak from your father," Granny added, but even that was tantamount to saying "Very well, have it your own way." Which was precisely what she did say. "Very well," she sighed, "have it your own way." Then, to avoid sounding unduly compliant and to assert a grandmother's authority, she said sternly: "Stay here, then." But it didn't sound stern to Katharina's ears; it sounded like a cheerful refrain. Stay here, then . . . it had a lovely ring! She felt like the flea in Alsace. And even when Granny added a sterner remark, a nasty one designed to make it clear that she ought to be severe and angry with such a wilful child, Katharina found it pleasing to the ear. Granny said: " Kaspar and I will go without you, then."

Well, Katharina thought, they were welcome to go without her, it was the ideal solution. Then she wouldn't have to attend to her brother all the time – help him to wee and get him drinks of water – and she wouldn't have anyone to look after but herself. Nothing could blight her elation, not even when Margret called from upstairs that Didi could mind the baby for her, because Didi was the Katharina the others knew, the one who was helping Kaspar on with his cape, whereas deep inside her was the real Katharina, the one known only to herself, who sat on a golden globe with a silver clasp in her hair and knew precisely what to do . . . and *that* Katharina had won the day.

18

"COMING?" SHE SAID TO THE SHEEP STANDING JUST inside Granny's bedroom. They were the only doll's house animals made of fir cones, not bones, and for legs they had matchsticks. They gave off a faint scent of resin.

The sheep bleated but didn't budge. As if they didn't know they had no business in Granny's bedroom!

"Then I'll have to get Sultan," said Katharina. She fetched the dog, which had remained on the steps behind the stove after driving a cow up them. She placed him at the rear of the little flock, and one sheep after another condescended to move with the black sheepdog occasionally snapping at their hind legs. Katharina, shuffling along on her knees, picked up the animals and put them down at brief intervals, and in this way the flock slowly approached the foot of the stove.

Baby Anna, who was lying in a basket beside the stove, started to cry when the dog barked at a straggler. This was a nuisance because the sheep hadn't reached their destination yet, and Katharina wanted them to join the farmer's family.

"Look out for the hawk," she cried. Snatching up two sheep at once, she deposited them on the stove and said "Good sheep!" in a deep voice: the farmer had spoken. Then she did the same with the rest of the animals until the whole family and all its livestock were assembled on top of the stove, and people, sheep, pigs, cows, horses, goats and chickens were peering over the edge into the parlour beneath.

Katharina took little Anna from her basket. It was incredible how heavy a baby of her age could be. She sat down at the table and put her on her lap. Anna seemed to like that. She stopped crying, at least, and gazed round the room.

"They're all up there," said Katharina, pointing to the doll family. "They went looking for their chickens and now they've found them. See the chickabiddies?"

But Anna looked down at the floor, not up at the stove.

"The chickens were frightened of the rocks. They ran all the way up there. Right up there, see?" She pointed again at the top of the stove. When Anna still wouldn't look in the right direction she took hold of her chin, turned her to face the stove, and tilted her head back. Anna started to cry, twisted her little head away, and braced her feet against Katharina's thighs. Katharina let go and Anna promptly stared at the floor again.

"All right, look wherever you like," said Katharina.

She supposed a baby of Anna's age was really too small to obey instructions. There were many times when she couldn't even get Kaspar to do what she wanted, and he was four already. It was two hours since he'd set off down the track to the village, hand in hand with his grandmother and looking like a dwarf in his cape. Katharina had watched them go from the parlour window. Granny was using her free hand to hold the big umbrella and the basket, whose lid she'd fastened with two catches. Züsi had fiercely resisted imprisonment, and she could still be heard mewing as they disappeared into the trees. Margret had managed to capture her on the top floor, but not without receiving a scratch on the hand which Granny doctored with schnapps. Kaspar had been reluctant to go when he saw that his sister was being allowed to stay behind.

"Want to stay here too," he'd announced, sitting down on the little shoe bench in his cape.

"The very idea!" said Granny, promptly hauling him to his feet again, and he gave in.

They were bound to have reached the Meur and seen the baby by now. Would Papa and Mama really name her Euphemia, the way Granny wanted? When she was wrapping up the brooch, Granny had called her Euphemia as matter-of-factly as if she'd been christened that a long time ago. Perhaps she ought to have gone with them after all, Katharina reflected, if only to say she preferred the name Verena. They wouldn't have listened to her, though, so it was just as well she'd stayed behind, playing with the dolls by herself and keeping an eye on little Anna, who was staring at the floor again instead of up at the stove.

It wasn't until she looked at the floor herself that she saw what had attracted Anna's attention: the little black sheepdog was still standing there waiting for a hawk, or a hand pretending to be a hawk, to carry it up to join the farmer's family and their livestock.

"Poor Sultan," said Katharina. "Were you left behind all on your own?"

She put both arms around little Anna in readiness to get up and replace her in the basket, but before she could do so Anna started crying again.

"You'll have to wait," she told the dog. "I'll put you with the others in a minute." She gently dandled Anna on her knee. The baby quietened but went on staring at the floor. "Do you want to play with the bow-wow?" Katharina asked. Without waiting for an answer, she put Anna down on her tummy, right in front of the bone dog. At once, the baby let out a piercing wail. Katharina reluctantly picked her up again and tried to sit her down with her back against the stove, but she keeled over, unable to right herself, and started to cry. So Katharina sat down herself with her back to the stove, spread her legs, settled Anna between them, and dangled her plaits in front of the baby's nose. Anna watched them at first, then reached out and caught hold of one in her tiny fist. When she tugged at the plait, Katharina gave a little cry of pain and the baby released it. Katharina tossed back her plaits and cautiously reached for the dog.

Just then the house was hit by a gunshot that set every window pane rattling. Katharina heard Margret cry out upstairs. She laid little Anna down and ran to the parlour window. A dense, evil-looking cloud was rising above the Plattenberg, and its source was neither fire nor gunfire. Something immense must have broken off, something bigger than a slab of rock: a piece of the mountain itself.

Anna was crying. Katharina turned, picked her up, and carried her over to the window. Hurried footsteps could be heard on the stairs.

Margret burst into the parlour a moment later. "What on earth was that?" she asked.

"A piece of the mountain broke off," Katharina told her, pointing to the cloud of dust.

"Surely not," said Margret. She joined Katharina at the window.

The thunderous sound reverberated from every rock face and went rolling down the valley. It sounded like a giant playing skittles.

Silence slowly returned. A light breeze drove fine raindrops against the window panes. The sparrows that had been clamouring outside all afternoon had fallen silent. The cloud of dust that marked the spot was steadily expanding. Behind it there must be a big bald patch on the mountain. They would have to wait until the cloud dispersed before they could see anything.

"Let's hope they'll be back soon," Margret muttered. She sighed. "It's lucky Paul went to Steinibach."

Katharina tried to remember where Steinibach was: beyond the village and a long way from the Plattenberg.

"But Granny's down in Untertal," she said.

"She may be on her way back by now."

"Yes," said Katharina, "and perhaps she's bringing Mama and Papa and the rest of them with her."

"Don't be silly," Margret said curtly. "Women who've just had babies don't go climbing mountains."

"What if they carry her?"

"It can't be that bad."

Anna whimpered in Katharina's arms.

"Here," said Margret. She unbuttoned her blouse and held the baby to her breast, but Anna pushed her away with her fists and refused to drink.

"All right, don't," said Margret. She went over to the basket beside the stove and put Anna in it, but this provoked such a series of despairing cries that she picked her up again and proceeded to rock her in her arms.

"A fire on the hearth and a roof overhead, and Baby's all cosily tucked up in bed," she sang in a low, cajoling voice. And Katharina, who was still standing at the window, fervently hoped that the Meur's roof was intact, and that none of those horrid rocks had rolled down on the house in which all save herself were doubtless assembled at this moment – Mama and Papa and Anna and Regula and Jakob and Kaspar and the newborn baby, whatever her name was – because Sunday was the day you stayed at home, at least when you got back from church and Sunday school, and as a rule sat down to a good midday meal. Mama sometimes roasted a joint, and for the children she put a loaf in the baking tin as well and poured the gravy from the joint over it so that it became wonderfully soft and tasted just like meat. Children's roast, they called it, and it was so delicious that her big sister Anna, who wasn't a child any more, liked it almost better than the real roast.

On Sunday afternoons Papa and Mama had to mind the taproom, and in fine weather the children were allowed to play outside, but when it rained they had to go upstairs and keep quiet. That presented problems because Kaspar, in particular, always wanted to be kept occupied. The only toy they all liked and fought over was the rocking horse, but Kaspar's games were not the same as Katharina's. Uncle Johannes had once brought them some nice wooden bricks from the joiner's workshop. Kaspar liked to sit in the passage and pile them up on top of each other, but he burst into tears whenever one of his towers or houses collapsed and you had to interrupt your own game to help him rebuild them.

Since going to school Katharina had been allowed to play "Guess what?" with Jakob and Regula, a game she was very fond of. They would all sit on the bed and one of them would think of something – the sun, for instance – and the others had to find out what it was by asking questions. "Is it alive?" was a good question, and so were "Is it made of wood?" and "Is it made of stone?" Sometimes it was also worth asking "Can you touch it?". You couldn't touch the sun, after all, and the same applied to the wind or a cloud. Each question was ticked off on a slate, and the person who thought of the hardest thing, the one that had the most ticks against it, was the winner. Jakob often thought of stupid things like his underpants, and Regula tended to think of children she went to school with, and Katharina had once won a round by thinking of the baby in their mother's tummy. The others almost failed to guess it, because it was alive but impossible to touch. Regula and Jakob surpassed one another in their wild conjectures, which ranged from eagles to whales, and Katharina giggled proudly as she shook her head and made yet another tick on the slate until, with her 55th question, Regula finally hit the mark. Katharina well remembered how her sister had blushed when asking it.

It suddenly occurred to her that she had forgotten something. When Margret went off to the kitchen with the baby in her arms, Katharina crawled over to the bone dog and walked him, little by little, to the stove. No hawk scooped him up and carried him there, not this time, because Sultan was a watchdog as well as a sheepdog. He had to have sharp eyes in case one of his charges got lost.

Margret came back into the parlour. She looked around, startled.

"Where are you, Katharina?"

Katharina had just reached the farmer's family on top of the stove. She put Sultan down beside the sheep. "Safe at last," she whispered in his ear.

19

KATHARINA WAS SITTING CROSS-LEGGED ON THE PARLOUR table with little Anna in her arms. Margret had lit the kitchen range, and she could hear the crackle of the flames and smell the scent of resin that was gradually pervading the room.

With the baby propped on her right hip, one arm around it and the other hand supporting its chest, Katharina was showing it the view from the window.

"Look, see that grey patch in the middle of the trees? That's where it all fell down."

The cloud that had obscured the area until a quarter of an hour ago had slowly dispersed. A big gash ran right across the mountainside. Katharina could clearly see where the rock had broken off, and she could guess where it had plunged into the trees. That must be the crevice the wood-cutters had talked about.

"You see that dark crack? That's the Great Chlagg."

Anna made another attempt to grab one of her plaits. Katharina rocked her head to and fro, chanting: "The Great Chlagg, the Great Chlagg . . ."

Margret appeared in the doorway. "What was that?"

"You can see the mouth of the Great Chlagg."

"Where?"

"Ouch!" Katharina exclaimed. Little Anna had caught hold of a plait and was tugging at it. She detached the tiny fingers and tossed her head so that both plaits hung down her back, then pointed to the cleft.

"You think that's it?" said Margret.

Katharina nodded. Margret surprised her sometimes. What did she mean, "think"? Of course that was it.

"I always thought it was further up."

There it was again: "I thought . . ." Katharina resolved to think as little as possible when she grew up.

"No, that's it," she said firmly, "and it won't hold much longer."

She gave a start. She hadn't uttered that last sentence. It must have been the other Katharina.

"How would *you* know?" said Margret. "It'll hold for as long as it chooses to. I'm going to make us a fresh pot of tea." And she went back into the kitchen, which soon gave out a medley of noises: saucepans and mugs and jugs clattering, water being ladled, the range being stoked.

Katharina thought over what her other self had just said.

If it was true, and she didn't doubt it – if it was true, then everyone in Untertal ought to get out as fast as possible. I hope they do, she thought, I hope they do, I hope they run for their lives. Dear God, please make them run, or our family at least. Old Jaggli and Young Jaggli would probably stay put in spite of the rumbling rocks, or if they did decide to leave they'd first bundle up their clothes and the stocking containing their savings and close the shutters so the window panes wouldn't shatter the way they had at the Martinsloch, and they'd probably stop to lock up the house but go inside again because they couldn't find the key. But by this time Papa would surely have had a word with Beat Rhyner, who didn't trust the mountain either – he'd seen the Great Chlagg for himself, after all – and they were bound to realize they ought to get out, and they could carry Mama downstairs and put her on the sledge – Papa was probably hauling it out of the tool shed at this very moment – and Anna would have to carry the newborn baby and Jakob and Regula would run on ahead with Kaspar between them, not towards the iron bridge but in the opposite direction, towards the meadow. And Katharina could picture Lobe galloping off with her tail in the air, bellowing, and Hans-Kaspar sprinting up from the village and across the iron bridge because he'd heard the crash and seen some houses buried and wanted to help – to help his beloved Anna first and foremost – and Johannes would be there too, and although a few children would be running away from Untertal, whole groups of men and women would be running towards it, and Katharina hoped they'd get there in time to warn the people and get them out, because she could already see how the trees at the very top beside the raw gash in the mountainside were toppling over backwards into the Chlagg, which simply swallowed them like some voracious mountain giant, and how the whole of the forest below the cleft was sliding into the valley and how the trees and rocks were somersaulting downwards, and she couldn't understand why the whole process was unfolding in such absolute silence, as if it weren't really happening at all. But now, at long last, the mountain remembered that it had to thunder in order to be real, and it thundered and rumbled and raged and roared and the black sheepdog started how-ling – or was it Nero outside in his kennel? – and Katharina called "Margret!" but Margret had gone to the stable or the lavatory – the kitchen door had creaked a moment ago – and Margret couldn't help the people in Untertal anyway, and they would have to escape by them-selves, it was high time, and perhaps they would make it after all because the Chlagg could still be clearly seen beside the new rockfall that was vanishing in a whirlwind of dust, so perhaps there would still be time if Anna handed the newborn baby to Hans-Kaspar so he could run on ahead while she saw to the younger ones, and the sledge with Mama on it was already being hauled along with Papa pulling in front and Granny pushing behind, and the people around them were crying out in terror because they realized at last that their lives were in danger, and they were running off in all directions, not only towards the iron bridge, where the blacksmith was waiting with his wagon, but up towards the Düniberg as well, and the younger ones overtook their elders and urged them on, but they stood there coughing and gasping because the dense cloud of dust from the rock-fall had got into their noses, mouths and eyes – yet they mustn't stop, not for a moment – and Katharina now saw what the other Katharina had known all along, and she called to Margret, who had reappeared in the parlour, that some-thing was coming down on Untertal and the Great Chlagg wouldn't hold for much longer – it would bring the whole mountainside down with it – and she would have put her hands over her ears if she hadn't been holding the baby, because she didn't want to hear the sound that would come from the Plattenberg at any moment. And sure enough, here it came, preceded by a gust of wind that almost flattened the trees below the house and shook the walls so violently that the window panes rattled and tiles fell off the roof. And the valley was filled with a crash like a hundred thunderstorms at once, and through the huge cloud of dust that now covered the whole of the Plattenberg she saw a massive, pitch-black rock go soaring through the air like a piece of rotten wood, high above Untertal, and she knew that all was lost, and that she would never see any of the family again, neither Papa nor Mama nor Kaspar nor Regula nor Jakob, and that Anna would never again kiss Hans-Kaspar behind the inn, and that Anna would never explain the secret of men and women to her, and that Granny had walked down the track but would never climb it again, and that Züsi and the hens had sought refuge up here in vain, and she would never again be sent into the big wine casks or hang up paper chains for music and dancing at the Meur, because the Meur was now, at this very moment, being engulfed by a stone flood that would never recede, and the Rhyners would not escape either, and not even a shutter would remain of either of the Jagglis' houses, and there would be no more fetching eggs from old Elsbeth, and young Elsbeth wouldn't die of her goitre, and Old Jaggli would never light his pipe again, and Johannes would repair no more salt jars and make no more coffins and wouldn't even need one himself, because the flood would bury them all for evermore and wash over the Sernf and swallow the iron bridge and entomb not only the blacksmith and the horseshoe he'd threatened to nail to her foot but also all the children she'd played blind man's buff with, and she would never again tell that dunce Anna Elmer the answer to six minus five . . . and only cheeky Oswald, who so often missed school, would miss the Flood as well, because he'd sneaked off to Matt with some other boys. And Kleophea's christening party would also be engulfed, and she would help a few of the children out of the window before being swept away with her baby in its white christening robe. And the midwife with the red hair-ribbon who had just hauled Katharina's baby sister out of Mama's tummy would hand little Fridolin to her husband, only to be struck down by the Great Flood's furthest eddies. And not even Blind Meinrad, sitting at the window in his thick Suvorov cap, who was bound to have heard all the ominous noises in good time, would escape, because there was no one to show him which way to go.

And the other Katharina saw all these things while Katharina herself, with Margret silently resting a hand on her shoulder and the rescued dolls gazing down in dismay at the valley below, was sitting on the parlour table with little Anna, who now had a plait in either hand and was tugging them so hard that Katharina's head jerked to and fro and the scene before her eyes became blurred into a thunderous black cloud; and she knew that somewhere beyond it the other Katharina was sitting on a golden globe, and that from now on she would need all her strength not to lose her.

Author's Note

KATHARINA RHYNER-DISCH DIED, AGED 85, AT "MEISSENBODEN", Elm, in 1959. She had two sons, one daughter, and numerous grandchildren and great-grandchildren.

I should like to thank all those in Elm, Glarus and elsewhere who assisted me in my quest for the real-life Katharina and thus enabled me to reinvent her in the foregoing pages.